MOON RAIDERS

Wayne Creek is a family town, not overly prosperous. However, when Samuel Lane arrives with his own enrichment in mind, change is anticipated. Though the town might find affluence through him, it would also become dangerous, with the dregs of the West flooding in . . . Standing alone against Lane is Jeb Tierney. The scales of justice seem to be loaded against him — and yet nothing is quite as it seems. Will Lane, after all, get his much-deserved comeuppance?

SKEETER DODDS

MOON RAIDERS

Complete and Unabridged

LINFORD
Leicester

First published in Great Britain in 2007 by
Robert Hale Limited
London

First Linford Edition
published 2008
by arrangement with
Robert Hale Limited
London

British Library CIP Data

Dodds, Skeeter
   Moon raiders.—Large print ed.—
   Linford western library
   1. Western stories
   2. Large type books
   I. Title
   823.9'2 [F]

   ISBN 978–1–84782–089–1

Published by
F. A. Thorpe (Publishing)
Anstey, Leicestershire

Set by Words & Graphics Ltd.
Anstey, Leicestershire
Printed and bound in Great Britain by
T. J. International Ltd., Padstow, Cornwall

This book is printed on acid-free paper

1

The red glow at the bedroom window woke Jeb Tierney, and he knew instantly what the glow represented.

Fire!

'What is it, Jeb?' his wife Martha asked drowsily, as he leapt from the bed.

'The barn's on fire.' Martha Tierney came instantly awake, joining her husband in a scramble to get dressed. 'Stay in the house!' he ordered her curtly.

'But you'll need help, Jeb.'

'By the intensity of that glow,' he indicated the window, 'there's nothing left to help with.'

'But the barn's full of our crops.'

'Was,' he growled, going to the door.

'Be careful,' Martha warned. 'Go slowly, until you know who's out there.'

'They'll have long gone.'

'They?'

'The Moon Raiders, of course, woman.'

On his way outside, Tierney grabbed a rifle from the gun-rack just inside the cabin door, but knew that there would be nothing to shoot at, the Moon Raiders came and left with the stealth of a ghost. The full moon would have lit the yard with its benign yellow glow, except that the angry red of the burning barn predominated. During the previous two full moons he had waited and watched, but the Moon Raiders had not appeared, and neither had his neighbours seen them. So, foolishly, he had believed that the curs who made up the Moon Raiders had scattered and he had dropped his guard. However, obviously that was exactly what they wanted folk to think.

The Moon Raiders, as the devils who raided in the middle of the night under the light of a full moon were called were, Tierney had no doubt, the agents of one Samuel Lane, outwardly a saloon-keeper, but his brash wealth was evidence that his coffers were swollen by interests other than what the income from a saloon would bring him. The story was that he was a shrewd investor, and no doubt he had cunning in spades. But seeing that he was little more than a full turn of seasons in Wayne Creek, which had begun modestly, everyone was at a loss as to how he had accumulated the fortune he had in such a short span of time.

'I need proof, Tierney!' had been Marshal Frank Jackson's response to Tierney's complaint of a couple of months before when his well had been fouled during the night, and he had suggested to the marshal that he should go and ask Samuel Lane about it. But then he had been expecting too much by far to get a response other than the cold-shoulder he had received from the so-called marshal of Wayne Creek, seeing that his fortunes seemed to be rising in line with Lane's, not as spectacularly, but still way beyond what a marshal's pay could enrich a man by, even the most moderate of men. 'It ain't good enough to say that everyone knows, Tierney. That's heresay, not proof.'

He would still go to town tomorrow and complain again, but nothing would change. Samuel Lane wanted the valley to lay track across it for a rail spur to town. It was the only way the spur could reach the town within the budget that the railroad company had allotted. Lane knew, as everyone else did, that whoever owned the land over which the track would run, would have a mighty handsome bank balance. The railroad bounty divided, collectively, the farmers and ranchers of the valley would not be enriched and, besides, most would prefer to have land than cash. However, any one man owning the valley would have the railroad negotiators over a barrel and gain handsomely. Whereas, were twenty or more ranchers and farmers to split the pot, their individual take would come no way near the compensation they would need to up roots and resettle, except maybe on cheaper land nearer the desert where the quality of soil dropped dramatically and grass would not be much more than weed.

Only a short time before, at a meeting called by Tierney, the farmers and ranchers had voted to stand together to stymie Samuel Lane's ambitions. However, within days, Lane had coaxed some occupants of the valley with cash, and others he had moved on by coercion, and more, tired of the continuous trouble Lane's Moon Raiders gave them, had just given up.

'I'll double my offer, Tierney,' Lane had proposed to him, only days previously when he had visited town to pick up supplies. 'Can't be fairer than that.'

'My land ain't for sale, Lane,' had been Tierney's steely-eyed reply. 'And I'll ask you to take note of the new signs forbidding trespass that I've put up; signs that will give me the right to shoot any man setting foot on my property without an invite to do so.'

'Pretty soon you'll be standing alone, Tierney,' Lane had sneered. 'Your neighbours are seeing sense and settling with me.'

'I'm afraid, Lane, that your idea and mine of *fair*, ain't the same.'

He recalled Darkie Clark's sly grin, so called because of his mixed blood. 'Don't you want an easier life, Tierney,' he'd said, in the quietly threatening way he did. 'Hard work makes for young widows.' The young gunnie's grin became a snigger.

Jeb Tierney dropped the sack of flour he was loading and grabbed Clark by the shirt front, hauling him toe to toe. 'You, Clark,' he growled, 'I'll take particular delight in cutting down, if I see you on my land.'

Clark's sneer remained in place.

'Maybe you won't see me,' he paused, 'until it's too late for you, sodbuster.'

Tierney tightened his grip on the

gunslinger's shirt.

'Easy, Tierney,' Frank Jackson had intervened, springing to Darkie Clark's assistance. 'Ain't no call to start trouble which you might come out the wrong end of.'

'Still licking butt, Marshal,' Tierney had angrily flung back.

Goaded, Jackson's hand dropped to his sixgun, and he may very well have drawn had Samuel Lane not stepped between the so-called lawman and the sodbuster to pour oil on troubled waters, conscious no doubt of the gathering on the board-walk which had begun with a couple of curious on-lookers, but had mushroomed to a sizeable crowd during the couple of minutes of acrimonious exchanges between Lane and Tierney, divided fairly evenly the farmer reckoned between Lane's supporters and opponents.

'I'm sure Mr Tierney didn't mean any offence, Marshal Jackson,' he said, with snake-oil smoothness. 'These are tense times.' His eyes swept the crowd. 'Wayne Creek is at a crossroads. There's the chance to grab prosperity you folk never dreamed would be yours. Or there's the chance to stand still and see the town die as the railroad makes our neighbours prosperous. Because that's what will happen, sure as night follows day, if there is any further dalliance. The railroad men are impatient cusses. Their business is laying track as fast as they can. And if Wayne Creek don't want it, they'll lay it northwards to Kelly's Crossing and Huston Gorge and other towns. And if that happens, all that will be left around here is drifting tumble weed.'

Lane, quick as snake-spit, had not lost a second to grab a platform to promote his cause, and sow the seeds of doubt and division in the community that had been his stock-in-trade since the moment he had stepped off the coach a year ago.

Some of Wayne Creek's citizens reckoned that the railroad would be a blessing that would bring full and plenty to the town, and there was good cause for believing so on the evidence of what had happened to other towns into which the railroad had run track. However, others feared that the homely values and trouble-free living they had had up to now would vanish when the railroad would bring the dregs of the territory and indeed the wider West to their door; dregs like brothel-keepers and gamblers, outlaws and gunslingers, the kind of unwelcome folk that followed the track because it offered comfort of travel that horseriding or stagecoaches did not, and cash-filled pockets to be robbed in one way or another. A no-good, faced with riding the back-breaking trails leading to Wayne Creek, would blanch at the hardship involved. But there would be no such labour in riding the train. Other towns had got prosperity, of that there was no doubt, but they had also got trouble a-plenty. And the decision for any town offered a spur was the same; a choice between a clean family town with relatively meagre living. Or a bustling, money-spinning town that never shut down, and one in which the respectable and peace-loving rubbed shoulders with the greedy and lawless who ran the saloons and whorehouses that attracted the scum of the territory, whose ill-gotten gains were the bedrock of that new prosperity.

Jeb Tierney stood looking at the smouldering rubble that had been his barn, his harvest a charred mess, and his anger knew no bounds.

'Where are you going, Jeb?' his wife fretted when shortly after first light he saddled up.

'To kill that bastard Lane,' he growled, his face dark and scowling.

'You're no gunhand, Jeb,' she said, her fretting reaching new heights. 'Lane will be surrounded by hardcases, who'll only be too glad to kill you.'

'Don't you realize, woman,' he barked, 'we're ruined!'

'We can start again, Jeb,' she pleaded.

'There'll be another harvest come along.'

'You don't get it, do you, Martha,' Tierney said. 'There won't be another harvest to fill another barn. Lane wants us out of the valley. And if we don't go, sooner or later we'll catch lead, if I don't stop him in his tracks right now.'

'Go talk to Marshal Jackson, Jeb,' Martha Tierney pleaded.

'Hah!' he scoffed. 'That's like going to Satan to complain about a demon's wrong-doing!'

'Then if you must go, I'm going with you, Jeb.'

'No, you ain't. It'll be job enough to watch myself, without having to look out for you. If you're a widow you'll find out soon enough.'

Martha Tierney watched her husband ride away, praying that it was not for the last time.

Jeb had no sooner crested the hill to the south of the cabin, when Martha Tierney became aware of a rider approaching from the hills behind the cabin. She was gripped by instant panic. She was a woman alone, and that was no way to be in a more or less lawless territory.

2

Martha hurried inside the house to get a rifle, conscious of how useless her action was, seeing that she had never learned guncraft beyond the most basic form. But she knew the persuasion value of a pointed rifle. However, pointing a rifle and convincing the man it was pointed at of one's ability to use it with precision was not an easy art, and would be an utterly useless exercise if the man riding in had come up the outlaw trails from Mexico; the kind of man who would instinctively know how bereft of gun know-how she was.

She thought briefly about going outside to talk back into the house, to give the stranger the impression that she was not alone. It was an old ruse, but it still worked sometimes. But if the man was as instinctive as she suspected he might be, he'd quickly see through her shenanigans and quickly reach the conclusion that the rifle she was holding was as effective as a fly swatter. Anyway, he had probably seen Jeb ride off.

Martha looked in the mirror and practised her stance, trying to make it as threatening as she could, but no matter how she postured she still could not, to her way of thinking, strike anything near a purposeful pose. She simply looked awkward and gawky — someone to amuse rather than scare. Maybe if she hid, the stranger would ride by and leave her be? Unlikely though, Martha concluded. More likely that he would see easy pickings and take what he wanted. Besides, he had probably seen her from the higher ground when she had waved Jeb off. No, she would have to face up to the stranger. There was nothing else she could do.

Toting the rifle, Martha Tierney went outside, praying that the heart-stopping fear within her would not be justified.

The stranger was riding into the yard.

'Howdy, ma'am,' he greeted Martha affably. But that was nothing to go by, she reminded herself. Some of the most notorious renegades riding western trails could be as smooth as silk and as sweet as wild honey when it suited their needs. 'Name's Hadley, ma'am,' he informed her. 'That would be Jess Hadley.'

The name meant nothing to her, but she thought that it should.

'What is it you want?' Martha enquired brusquely.

Jess Hadley grinned. 'No need to parley under the threat of a rifle,' he said. 'I mean you no harm.'

'What is it you want?' Martha repeated, making no move to redirect the Winchester from Hadley's person.

'I figured that I'd ask you if I could fill my canteen from your well, ma'am,' he said.

'Town ain't far more to go.' Martha Tierney wondered if she was taking a too unneighbourly stand; a stand that

15

might goad Hadley and make him mean. But all she could think of was getting rid of the stranger. 'You won't die of thirst before then,' she added.

'Ain't very neighbourly, are you, ma'am,' Jess Hadley stated, his tone grim. 'Even a dog would get a drink of water.'

'The well's fouled,' Martha lied.

Hadley's gaze went troublingly behind her to the house. 'You here all alone, ma'am?'

'Ain't none of your business, mister!'

'This can be dangerous country for a woman alone.'

'I can take care of myself.'

'Brave words,' he said, his grin wide. 'But I'm guessing that you're about as handy with that 'Chester as a cripple is at dancing.'

Martha Tierney's heart threatened to leap right out of her mouth. 'You'll only find out you're wrong when and if you try something,' she intoned.

Jess Hadley's grin became full blown laughter. 'I guess I'll manage my thirst until I reach town, ma'am.'

'That would be the wisest thing to do,' Martha replied.

Jess Hadley looked beyond Martha to the ruined barn. 'Trouble?'

'None of your darn business,' Martha replied brusquely.

Hadley swung his mare. 'Ain't welcome here, hoss,' he said. 'But I'd be obliged if you'd point the way to Wayne Creek, ma'am.'

'The northern end of the valley. Can't miss it. Got business there?'

'Yes. With a man called Samuel Lane.' Martha Tierney's heart staggered. 'I hear he's hiring right now. You know Mr Lane?'

'I know him,' Martha spat. 'Wish I didn't though. You'd better git right now!'

'Don't know what I've done to rile you so, ma'am,' Hadley said. 'But I'm sure sorry.'

'I don't want your apology, just the back of you.'

'Let's hit the trail, hoss,' Hadley said.

Martha Tierney watched Hadley out of sight, but did not allow herself to relax. If he was on his way to hire out the low slung Colt. 45 he wore to Samuel Lane, it meant that he had a rotten streak in him, and probably a bag of equally rotten tricks to choose from, like men of his kind always had. And yet, though admitting to being rotten by seeking to join the Lane string of hardcases, there was something about Hadley that did not mark him down as a typical Lane employee.

She kept watch for most of an hour, before going about the hundred and one chores needing her attention.

★   ★   ★

Jess Hadley was riding through a gorge when a bullet spun off a boulder near him. He dived for his sixgun, but a second bullet followed the first, bearing a message he fully understood. It said that the next one would go right between his eyes, if he put up any resistance. He reached for the sky to indicate that he had no such intention.

A short distance up ahead, a man toting a rifle stepped from behind twin boulders leaning on each other like Saturday night drunks.

'Toss your gunbelt, rifle too, mister,' he ordered Hadley. 'Blink and I'll blast you out of your saddle.'

'I'm giving you no argument,' Hadley said. 'But I'd sure like to know what I've done to have earned your ire, sir.'

'This gorge is on my land. You're trespassing, and that's reason enough for me,' the man said stonily.

'I didn't see any signs.'

'Haven't got them up across my land yet.'

'Then with no signs, you can't blame a man for wandering.'

'Who are you?' the man demanded.

'The name's Jess Hadley.'

'*Jess Hadley!*'

'I take it by that yelp that you know my rep?'

'I've heard of you,' Jeb Tierney

19

admitted. 'What're you doing in these parts?'

'Looking to hire out. I believe that a gent by the name of Samuel Lane is hiring. That so?'

'Lane will always find a place for a no-good like you, Hadley. Last I heard, you put a nineteenth notch on your gun down Sonora way a couple of months back?'

'Old news, friend,' Hadley bragged. 'Twenty it stands at. Now, are you going to use that rifle, or do I get to go on my way, mister?'

Jeb Tierney lowered the Winchester. 'I guess, working for Lane, we'll cross paths again, Hadley. Probably a whole lot sooner than you think.'

Jess Hadley's face hardened.

'You got the drop on me this time,' he barked, his mood mean. 'Next time I'll make damn sure you don't.'

'And you make damn sure that I don't catch you on my property again,' Tierney flung back with equal venom.

The man called Jess Hadley rode

away, his look changing from one of hard-bitten acrimony to one of frowning concern. Jeb Tierney's mood, too, changed from fiery defiance to apprehension. It was nothing new to find that Samuel Lane was adding yet another gunnie to his stable of hardcases. But Jess Hadley was no run-of-the-mill no-good like the men Lane already had on his payroll, Hadley was one of the West's ace gunslingers, a man who rode in the company of the Grim Reaper every day. On his own, he would be more than enough to handle, but teamed up with Darkie Clark, no mean gunslick himself, Lane would have in his employ a ruthless duo who would, for a pocket full of dollars, do anything he wanted done including callous murder.

Shaken, Tierney would much have preferred to turn tail and not go to town to challenge Lane in his lair. But he knew that turning tail quickly became a habit that sent a man down an ever slippery slope to cowardice, to live a life of boot licking. Such a life was not for him. And, besides, if someone did not stand up to Lane now, before long no one in town or the valley would dare to. And it was out of such fear that tyrants were born.

Continuing on his journey, Jeb Tierney's thoughts were of his wife Martha. Ten years they had been married and still childless. Sometimes he had been bitter about that, until he had the courage to admit to himself that their lack of issue might be his fault and not Martha's. Lack of children was always blamed on the woman, because a man's pride could not contend with the fault being in him. He knew that Martha blamed herself for the empty cradle, and to his shame he had not said anything to make her think otherwise, though there had been times when he had almost got round to talking about it. If he returned from his trip to town, he resolved that he would, and take his share of the burden for Martha's childlessness, and remove from their relationship the growing canker of discontent which had been driving them steadily apart.

Arriving at the edge of town, his ponderings were set aside on seeing the back-slapping going on outside the Bucking Buffalo saloon, Samuel Lane's den of iniquity. Darkie Clark, accompanied by Lane, were doing most of the back-slapping, the recipient of which was Jess Hadley. Marshal Frank Jackson, too, was doing his share of back-slapping.

'Didn't take you much darn time to hook up, did it, Hadley!' Jeb Tierney growled on reaching Lane and his cohorts.

Jess Hadley swung round.

'You again,' he snorted, and snarled: 'Looking for more gunplay, I hope.'

'Gunplay?' Lane enquired, his puzzled gaze flashing between Hadley and Tierney.

Hadley provided the explanation.

'Thought about shooting me for crossing his land, Mr Lane.'

'And Tierney's still sucking air,' Lane questioned the latest addition to his string of toughies. 'A tad unusual for a man who challenges Jess Hadley, ain't it?'

'I sometimes get in a generous mood,' Hadley said. 'But,' he settled steely grey eyes on Tierney, 'not very often. So don't prod me again, mister.' Jess Hadley's right hand massaged the butt of his sixgun.

Samuel Lane's confidence in his latest acquisition was restored. His mood became affable. 'Are you in town to accept my offer for your land, Tierney?' he enquired.

'I don't know how many times I have to tell you that my land is not for sale, Lane,' Jeb Tierney growled. 'But I'll tell you again anyway. It ain't for sale. Understood?'

'Thorny sort of fella, ain't ya,' Darkie Clark said, stepping forward, settling his guns on his narrow hips, dark eyes glowing with the expectation of trouble. 'I figure you should apologize to Mr

Lane for your sharp tongue, sodbuster.'

'Go to hell, Clark!' Tierney spat.

'Now what'cha go and do that for,' the hardcase drawled. 'Insultin' me, too.'

Lane rested against the saloon hitch-rail, enjoying the bargy between Tierney and Clark, his smile oily, his mean eyes full of a tense curiosity.

'Just in the nick of time before I go to press, Jeb,' a woman's voice said. Heads turned towards Lucy Galt, the owner, editor and general factotum of the Wayne Creek *Gazette*. 'If you step inside the office, we can do that interview now.'

Jess Hadley immediately sensed the tension the woman's appearance caused, especially in Samuel Lane.

'Interview?' Lane asked, straightening up from lounging against the saloon hitch-rail. 'What interview would that be?'

'Well now, Mr Lane,' Lucy Galt said, 'I guess you're going to have to buy a copy of the *Gazette* to find that out. You ready, Jeb?'

Hadley could see that Tierney was as taken aback as every other man at the woman's intervention, despite his best efforts to hide his surprise. She came and took Tierney's arm and pulled him along with her to the newspaper office.

'Damn busybody skirt!' Lane barked.

'Want me to get Tierney back here, Mr Lane?' Darkie Clark asked. 'Ain't fittin' that he should insult you and walk free.'

Lane obviously thought about giving the hardcase the go ahead, but held his anger in check with great difficulty.

'Who the heck is she?' Jess Hadley enquired of Lane.

Darkie Clark supplied the answer.

'Owner of the town newsrag,' he informed the newest member of Lane's riff-raff. 'Prints all sorts of lies 'bout Mr Lane,' he added. 'I just don't know how you keep your patience with that woman, boss.'

Having got control over his temper, Lane was generous in his response. 'Lucy Galt don't give me sleepless nights, Darkie. I've got more important things to worry about, like getting that rail spur to town.'

He turned to the newcomer.

'And with you on board now, Hadley,' his mood was confident, 'I reckon that my troubles in the valley are over and done with.'

Jess Hadley grinned and again massaged the butt of his plentifully notched sixgun. 'I guess you can count on that, Mr Lane.'

His gaze went after Jeb Tierney.

3

'What in tarnation are you talking about, Lucy?' was Jeb Tierney's angry question, as she guided him firmly towards the office of the *Gazette*. 'What interview?'

'The interview that just saved your hide, that's what interview,' Lucy Galt stated bluntly.

'I don't need your help to get out of a bind with Lane, young lady,' Tierney stated bluntly. 'I've got a crow to pluck with Lane. That's what I came to town for. The bastard burned down my barn during the night.'

He swung around to renew his challenge to Lane, but Lucy Galt swung him back in her direction.

'You must have a real hankering to die, Jeb Tierney,' she said, 'And bucking Samuel Lane the way you've been doing, is a surefire way of getting your wish. My late father — '

'Was murdered by Lane!' Tierney interjected.

'There's no proof of that,' Lucy said.

'The proof is right in here,' Jeb Tierney thumped his chest. 'If you'd only listen to your heart telling you.'

'My father was run down by a spooked wagon.'

'And who do you think did the spooking, huh? Darkie Clark, that's who. Because he was standing right alongside Sam Brennan's wagon outside the general store before the team bolted and ran your pa down.

'Ned was not fooled by Lane. He knew exactly the kind of sidewinder he is, and used his editorials to alert the town and hinterland to what the slick as silk newcomer to town was up to. That's why Lane had him killed.'

'Horses bolt for all sorts of reasons, Jeb,' Lucy Galt said.

Jeb Tierney shook his head wearily.

'Your pa's daughter, to be sure. Just as stubborn as your old man, aren't you. And, if you're not careful, you'll also meet with an *accident*. I've read your recent editorials, Lucy, and it might have been Ned who had penned them, which in my book means that somewhere inside that pretty red head of yours, you know that what I've just said about your pa's murder is true.

'You just won't let it come to the surface, because it's too darn horrible to think about.' Tears washed Lucy Galt's green eyes. 'I'm sorry my speech had to be so blunt and ornery, young lady,' Jeb Tierney said. 'But I've been telling you politely for long enough, and you keep on turning that famous Galt deaf ear all the time.

'Now, like I said, I've got a crow to pluck with Lane.'

'Stubborn, hah!' Lucy Galt flared. 'You've got the gall to call me stubborn!'

After an initial hostile reaction, Jeb Tierney grinned broadly. 'You know, I'd swear right now that your ma's standing in front of me, Lucy, rest her soul, good woman that she was. Taken too soon by fever. This town needs women like your ma; women who stood as bravely as any man to protect the good and revile the wicked.'

'Well, if you thought so highly of my ma and pa, and believe what you say yourself, then you'll not throw your life away pursuing a dented ego, Jeb Tierney! There's more than one way to skin a cat.'

Along the street Lane was furious.

'Thought Tierney would hand you the opportunity to kill him right on a plate, Darkie,' he growled.

'That woman's just like her pa, ain't she?' Clark grunted. 'Maybe she should have an accident just like her old man, Mr Lane.'

Lane's laughter was sly and humourless.

'These are dangerous times, Darkie. All sorts of strange things happen all the time.' He turned to Jess Hadley. 'You got anything to say, Jess?'

Hadley hunched his shoulders. 'Don't

feel that I've been around here long enough to reach any conclusions, Mr Lane.'

Samuel Lane considered the gunslinger for a long moment, before saying: 'Cautious man, Jess.'

'I've found that caution is just another word for good planning,' Jess Hadley drawled.

This time, Lane's laughter had more humour in it.

'Let's go inside and slake that thirst you must have worked up on the ride up out of Mexico, Jess,' he invited.

'Sure could do with oiling my throat,' Hadley said, falling in directly behind Lane and pushing Darkie Clark into second place. Clark's angry mean eyes showed his resentment at his new standing, and Hadley's mocking grin fanned that resentment to outright hatred.

'Once you've slaked your thirst, come back to the office,' Lane told Hadley. 'I want to fill you in on how I intend to shape things round here, Jess.'

Jess Hadley rubbed salt in Darkie Clark's wounds.

'Heck, my thirst can wait, Mr Lane. It ain't near as important as your business is.'

Lane swung around.

'You all hear that?' he questioned the men behind him. 'I suggest you fellas take a lead from Jess from now on.'

Darkie Clark's face turned snake ugly.

'Who's the new addition to Lane's payroll, Jeb?' Lucy Galt asked, craning her neck at the window to keep Jess Hadley in view for as long as she possibly could.

'A fella by the name of Jess Hadley, Lucy,' the sodbuster informed her glumly.

She swung around from the window. 'The gunfighter? That Jess Hadley?'

'That Jess Hadley,' Tierney confirmed, even grimmer still.

'Crikey!'

'I figure that Hadley is the last piece in Lane's plans to make this town, the valley and everyone in it kow-tow to him.'

'He must be stopped, of course,' Lucy Galt declared.

'Who's going to do the stopping,' Tierney said listlessly.

Not having an answer, Lucy Galt now shared in Jeb Tierney's glumness.

★　★　★

Samuel Lane was not reticent in telling Jess Hadley about his plans to take over the town and force out every rancher and farmer in the valley. 'If I own the land over which the railroad spur will run, I'll have a bank account bursting at the seams,' he said, his eyes greedy at the prospect. 'Then nothing can stop me from owning this town lock-stock-and-barrel. And with control of the town, I already own the marshal,' he boasted, 'we can make it a wide open town. So you can see, Jess, your future as my top gun is secured. And I can assure you right now that, like me, you'll end up with more money than you ever dreamed was in the world.'

'That's the kind of future I like to hear about, Mr Lane,' Hadley enthused.

'But it won't be easy,' Lane cautioned the gunfighter. 'Tierney will try and get others to follow his creed.'

Jess Hadley was dismissive of Jeb Tierney's worth.

'He'll run scared when the chips are down,' he predicted. 'Either that or he'll see the sense of throwing in his lot with you. I've seen it happen in a hundred towns, Mr Lane.'

Lane poured Hadley another whiskey.

'I don't think Tierney scares that easy, Jess,' he said. 'I've given him plenty to be scared about, and he hasn't flinched.' He picked up his own glass and sipped ponderously on the rye. 'And I'm not figuring on counting him in on my good fortune. A pie shared by too many isn't in my plans.'

His gaze on Jess Hadley was steady, inviting the gunfighter's input.

'Well, maybe a funeral would solve all our problems,' he drawled.

Samuel Lane chuckled. 'I just knew the second I set eyes on you, Jess, that you'd very quickly fit in to the outfit.'

* * *

'Now that I've got you in this office,' Lucy Galt said, 'let's go ahead and do that interview, Jeb. It only started out as a ruse to get you out of the mess you'd gotten yourself into, but it could serve a purpose.'

'What darn interview are you talking about, gal?' Jeb Tierney exclaimed.

'Let's use the *Gazette* to air your ideas about Lane and his plans for the town,' she enthused.

'You've gone loco!' Tierney yelped. 'Are you forgetting the price your pa paid for that editorial he wrote about Lane, the day before he was murdered?'

'No, I'm not,' Lucy Galt said quietly, her eyes filling. 'That's exactly why I want to do it, Jeb. You're right,' she admitted, 'Pa was murdered, and I've been burying my head in the sand ever since, finding all sorts of excuses to deny it, because I guess I was too scared to face up to confronting Samuel Lane and the evil he's infected this town with.'

Jeb Tierney snorted. 'Don't think, Lucy, that because you're a woman Lane will spare you. That cur would kill his own mother if it put an extra dollar in his pocket.'

'Don't you see, you can use the *Gazette* to start others thinking about Lane. You could talk all year and not reach as many as you will with one issue of the newspaper. And folk can sit in the quietness and privacy of their own parlours to do their thinking, unthreatened by Lane's hardcases.

'You've got to see the sense of it, Jeb,' she pleaded.

Jeb Tierney shook his head dismissively.

'I don't want any harm to come to you, Lucy,' he said. 'Bucking Lane is akin to stepping into a nest of vipers.'

'And what about Martha, Jeb? She'll be a long time in widow's weeds if you keep tangling with Lane.'

Jeb Tierney sighed, the world on his shoulders.

★ ★ ★

Darkie Clark was sullen of face and mood, his glance going continuously to the closed door of Samuel Lane's office where he was ensconced with Jess Hadley. His gut burned with resentment at how quickly he had been shunted into second place by Hadley's arrival. He was getting dangerously drunk and meaner of mind and spirit with each passing second.

'Looks like Hadley's got the boss's ear, Darkie,' said a small bow-legged man whose task in the overall run of things was to keep his ears and eyes open for possible trouble. 'It ain't fair, is it.'

Darkie Clark was under no illusion

about the man's motives. By nature he was a snake in the grass, and he was not going to miss out on the opportunity to rub Clark's nose in it. Despite knowing that it would be wise to ignore the jibe dressed up as friendliness, Clark swung the whiskey bottle he was pouring from at the man. The bottle broke on the man's forehead, but not satisfied with the damage it had done, Clark drew the jagged neck of the shattered bottle downwards over the man's right eye and onwards along his cheek to his jawline. The man howled in pain. Part of his right eye was hanging from the neck of the bottle, obscene evidence of the brutality done him. Not satisfied yet, Clark swung his boot against the man's ribs as he slumped to the floor, the snap of bone rang throughout the saloon. Then Darkie Clark grabbed the hapless man and pitched him through the saloon window on to the street, where he lay moaning.

The door to Samuel Lane's office swung open, Lane obviously furious at the disturbance in the saloon, not out of any sympathy for anyone on the receiving end of a bust up, but rather at the potential cost of any such conflagration. His gaze went instantly to Darkie Clark, because where he went trouble was never far behind.

'Benson started it,' was Clark's explanation. 'I tossed him out.'

'The cost of replacing that window comes out of your pay,' Lane said, neither enquiring or showing any sympathy for the man he saw curled up in the street through the shattered window whining like a wounded animal. He slammed the office door shut.

'Kind of witless ain't he, Darkie Clark,' Jess Hadley observed. 'Something like that brings a whole pile of bad publicity.'

Lane dropped into the chair behind his desk, his rage etched in every line of his face.

'Maybe Darkie Clark has outlived his usefulness, Jess, you reckon?'

'Maybe,' the gunfighter agreed.

'But he could be a heap of trouble if I kick him out.'

Hadley drew his .45 and rolled its chamber. 'Taking care of trouble is my bailiwick, Mr Lane,' he drawled lazily. 'You want Clark taken care of?'

'It might be an idea at that,' Lane said ponderingly.

'Of course, down the line, a gun as fast as Darkie Clark's could be useful,' Hadley observed.

'True,' Lane conceded.

'Maybe you should think about it, huh, boss?'

'Won't do any harm, I guess,' Samuel Lane agreed.

'And if you decide that Clark ain't worth the candle . . . ' Jess Hadley again rolled the chamber of his sixgun.

4

Lucy Galt was writing furiously, putting down on paper the text of what Jeb Tierney had to say when the bust-up at the Bucking Buffalo saloon interrupted. She joined Tierney at the door of the newspaper office to see the man whom Darkie Clark had wounded lying in the street, ignored by his cohorts for fear of incurring Clark's wrath and suffering the same fate or worse. The savaged man also had his cries going unheeded by those hurrying by on the boardwalks, fearful like Darkie Clark's cronies to become involved, though, if it were a wounded animal, they would not have hesitated.

'What's happening to this town, Jeb,' Lucy Galt said, about to go to the man's assistance, before Tierney restrained her.

'I'll go,' he said.

'*We'll* go,' she said determinedly.
Jeb Tierney smiled. 'Yes, ma'am.'

★　★　★

In Lane's office Jess Hadley suggested: 'Shouldn't someone see to — '

'None of our concern,' Lane replied brusquely. 'Benson's no longer on the Lane payroll.'

Jess Hadley seemed about to challenge his new boss, when the office door burst open.

'Didn't you ever learn to knock, Clancy!' Lane bellowed at the man who had burst in.

'Come look-see, Mr Lane,' he said, going to the window.

Lane and Hadley joined Clancy at the window, gawking, as if he was looking at the most extraordinary sight his eyes had ever witnessed. Lucy Galt was cradling Benson's head in her arms, drenched with his blood, while Jeb Tierney was imploring onlookers:

'Come help me take this man to the

doc's office.' And then berated them when no one came to render assistance: 'What kind of people are you? What's this town come to?'

'You know, I reckon if you were to make a show of compassion, Mr Lane, it would go down mighty well,' Jess Hadley suggested.

At first Lane saw no merit in his new henchman's suggestion, but on second thoughts he understood its worth.

'Slick thinking, Jess,' he congratulated Hadley. 'Can't do us any harm.'

Jess Hadley headed for the door.

'Hold up!' Lane commanded. 'You go,' he ordered Clancy.

'If the purpose of this exercise in hypocrisy is to cajole the townfolk, I figure that as I'm new in town I won't be carrying the kind of baggage that other men in your employ are, Mr Lane,' the gunfighter said.

Samuel Lane sized up Jess Hadley with a new respect.

'You're a real clever fella, Jess,' he intoned, and added just as Hadley was about to leave. 'Just don't get too smart, huh.'

★　★　★

Jeb Tierney looked up, scowling, on hearing Jess Hadley's offer of help.

'You can't take him to the doc's office on your own,' he told Tierney. 'And,' he looked to Lucy Galt, 'this fine lady's done more than her share already, I reckon.'

'I don't want any help from a Lane no-good!' Tierney barked.

'Have sense, Jeb,' Lucy scolded the sodbuster. 'Mr Hadley — '

'That'll be Jess, ma'am,' Hadley interjected.

'*Mr Hadley*,' Lucy emphasised, casting the gunfighter a withering look, 'has made a kindly offer, Jeb.' She continued: 'And the most important thing is to get this unfortunate man to Doc Brannigan's care.

'Even if it means pocketing your pride,' she added, when Tierney's reluctance to accept Jess Hadley's help remained steadfast.

'Grab his legs, Hadley,' Tierney said. 'I'll grab his shoulders. This is going to hurt real bad,' he warned the wounded man.

'Well, ain't that somethin', boys.' All eyes went to Darkie Clark staggering from the saloon, 'A big time gunfighter playin' nursemaid.'

The cronies with Clark, who were well into drunkeness sniggered.

'Mebbe you should go give Hadley a hand, Darkie,' one of his cohorts suggested.

'Ya think Miss Galt would give me a big kiss if'n I did, Spike?' Clark sneered.

'I reckon a whole lot more, Darkie, for carryin' that load of horse manure to the doc's office,' Spike chuckled, earning a loud guffaw from his partners.

When the laughter faded, Clark called out: 'Don't bother with the doc. Just take him to the cemetery.'

'I think you should show some respect in the presence of a lady, Clark.'

'You figger?' Clark growled in response to Jess Hadley's suggestion. He staggered down the saloon steps to the street, his face as mean as a riled polecat. 'Well, I don't, Hadley.' His hand dropped to hover over his sixgun. 'Now, if you're of a mind to try and make me . . . '

Samuel Lane watched intently from his office window, curious as to how the confrontation in the street would pan out.

'Darkie ain't too smart to go up agin Jess Hadley,' was Clancy's opinion. 'Not with all them notches on his gun. Want me to go out there and stop this?'

Lane shook his head. 'No. Haven't been this entertained in a long while.'

'Don't push this, Clark,' Jess Hadley warned.

'Ya know, Hadley, I think you're a lot of wind.' Clark shifted his stance. 'And I aim to prove it right here and now.'

'Will you two stop this nonsense,'

Lucy Galt commanded. 'This man needs to get to the doc's office.'

'The lady's got a point,' Hadley said. 'We can finish this later, Clark.'

'We'll finish it now, damn you!' the drunken gunnie roared. 'Or are you too yella, Hadley?'

Jess Hadley turned to Lucy Galt and Jeb Tierney. 'Looks like no one is going anywhere until I teach this loudmouth a lesson.'

'Loudmouth, huh!'

Darkie Clark dived for his sixgun, but before it cleared leather he was looking down the barrel of Jess Hadley's pistol. Clark blanched.

'Told ya,' the man with Samuel Lane pronounced, 'Darkie Clark's a dead man. I hear that Jess Hadley shows no mercy.'

Lane looked across the street to Jackson's office where the bought and paid for marshal was waiting for the signal to intervene, but Lane held back. He was still curious if, as Clancy said, Jess Hadley would show no mercy. If

Darkie Clark was the fodder to confirm that, then so be it.

To Lane and everyone else's surprise, Jess Hadley holstered his gun and hung a pile-driver on Darkie Clark's jaw that sent him crashing back painfully against the saloon hitch-rail. Hadley went and stood over him — Clark cowered.

'The next time you pull iron on me, I won't be as soft-hearted, Clark,' he promised. 'Now, let's get this man to the doc,' he told Jeb Tierney.

'I'll be knocked by a feather,' Clancy said in awe. 'Jess Hadley holdin' back on a killin'.' He shook his head. 'This darn country is goin' to the dogs, Mr Lane. It's so a man can't trust 'nother man to act in the way he's supposed to act no more.'

'Looks that way, Mike,' Samuel Lane concurred, deeply thoughtful.

'Jess Hadley's not as black as he's painted, is he?' Lucy Galt said, on arriving back in the office of the *Gazette*.

Jeb Tierney, as surprised as every

other man in town, did not answer Lucy Galt's question, simply because he was not sure of the answer. True, Hadley had acted out of character, but for what reason? And there just had to be a reason, of that Tierney was certain. Because he was a man who believed in leopards not changing their spots.

'Hadley's still got plenty of notches on his gun,' he reminded Lucy, perturbed by the soft way she spoke of Jess Hadley.

'A man can change, Jeb,' she said quietly, in fact almost dreamily.

'Don't doubt it. But not men of pure evil like Jess Hadley,' he opined.

'He could have justifiably killed Darkie Clark, Jeb.'

'Doesn't make sense,' Tierney said, after lengthy consideration. 'Because if, as you think, Jess Hadley has changed his ways, then why the heck did he go right back into Lane's nest of vipers?'

Lucy Galt's brow furrowed.

'That is strange, Jeb,' she conceded.

'Strange ain't the word for it, Lucy,'

Tierney said, shaking his head in wonder.

Looking beyond Tierney to the window behind him, Lucy said: 'You know, a whole pile of strangers have been arriving in town over the last couple of days, like that trio arriving now.'

Jeb Tierney turned to look at the men who were riding past the newspaper office, clean shaven and presentable.

'They look like good stock,' Tierney said, craning his neck to look after them as they headed for the town livery.

'They all do,' Lucy said.

'Any of them kow-towing with Lane?'

'Not one.'

Jeb Tierney rubbed his chin. 'Maybe they're railroad people? Scouting the terrain ahead of the track-layers.'

'Railroads are tight-fisted, Jeb. Can't see them spending good dollars on something that might never happen. And won't if the folk in the valley don't sell up to make way for the railroad. I figure that the railroad would have to have made a decision to run the spur here, before any railroad men would show up.'

'Then who the hell are they?'

Samuel Lane was also watching the arriving riders, but he had no questions, because he knew the answers.

5

Lucy Galt looked up when the office door opened and she paused in setting print for the next day's edition of the Wayne Creek *Gazette*, on seeing her surprise visitor.

'Howdy, ma'am,' Jess Hadley greeted her affably.

'What do you want, Mr Hadley?' she questioned him brusquely. She would have said, had she not known Hadley's killer reputation, that he had a winning smile. In fact the kind of smile that, had she not known who he was, would probably have sent her heart fluttering. That it still did, to a degree, was to her shame.

'Do you greet all your customers so curtly?' the gunfighter asked. 'If you do, I'm surprised you're still in business.'

'My question and its tone remain as

spoken, Mr Hadley. So I'd appreciate an answer.'

Jess Hadley took from his waistcoat pocket a sheet of paper and handed it over the counter to Lucy. It read:

Do you want your town to be left behind in the march to progress of this great country? Well it will be, if the railroad doesn't run a spur to it. Time is running out. A decision has to be made, and because I, Samuel Lane, have the good of this, my adopted town, at heart, I urge all of Wayne Creek's citizens and those in the valley to attend the meeting I have arranged in the saloon tomorrow night at 8 p.m., where each and every man can have his say, and cast his vote for or against this town having a future or not.

Signed:
Samuel Lane.

'Mr Lane would like that printed in tomorrow's edition of the Gazette, ma'am,' Hadley informed Lucy Galt.

'No room,' she replied.

'No room?'

'The paper's pages are already laid out and full, Mr Hadley. You tell Mr Lane that I'm truly sorry that I can't accommodate his advertisement.'

Jess Hadley chuckled.

'Do I also tell him that you're the prettiest liar I ever set eyes on.'

'How dare you!'

His chuckle became a laugh.

'Temper, too. Always fun in a woman, unless, of course a man has to suffer it.'

Lucy handed back Lane's advertisement.

'Good day, Mr Hadley. Sorry I can't stop to talk. But a newspaper doesn't print itself.' Lucy turned and went back to setting print.

'I think it would be a real bad mistake to refuse Mr Lane's business, Miss Galt,' Hadley said, his tone, to Lucy's ears, menacing.

Furious, she swung around. 'Are you

threatening me, Mr Hadley?'

'No, ma'am,' he was quick to reassure her. 'Simply pointing out that with Mr Lane's business growing all the time, the Gazette could benefit handsomely from his custom.'

He grinned his heart-fluttering grin again.

'Sorry if you got the wrong end of the stick just now.'

'I didn't,' Lucy stated boldy. 'And as for Lane's expanding business, I don't want to have a single blood-stained cent of it! Now you know, go and tell Lane that.'

'Must be the bad company you're keeping that's knocking good sense out of your head, Miss Galt. Maybe you should pick your company with more care.'

'I don't want or need your advice, Mr Hadley. Now that you found your way in here, I'm sure you'll have no difficulty in finding your way out again.'

'Mr Lane will surely be disappointed, and I guess angry, too.'

'That's his problem!'

'Well, you see, Miss Galt, if Mr Lane has a problem, it becomes my problem, and he'd expect me to take care of it before it riles him.'

Jess Hadley came round the counter. Lucy backed away.

'Get out!' she ordered. 'Or I'll call the — '

'Marshal,' Hadley sneered. 'I don't think that calling the marshal will do any good, do you, ma'am?'

Lucy Galt dived for a gun in the drawer of her desk. Hadley had no difficulty in dispossessing her of the Colt pistol. The tussle put her in close proximity to Hadley and, try as she might, she could not help feeling excited by the press of his athletically well-honed body against hers, leaving her breathless and shame-faced.

'You see, you've got to understand one thing, Miss Galt,' he said, his breath hot on her face. It's my job to see that Mr Lane gets what Mr Lane wants. Now . . . '

He handed back Lane's advertisement to Lucy.

' . . . I'm sure that you'll find space in the front page for this.' He strode to the door. 'Be sure to send Mr Lane the bill, Miss Galt. He'd hate for his reputation to be tarnished by not paying his debts.'

His parting chuckle left Lucy seething. But in fact what really had her dander up was her own racing heart beat. How could she possibly find even the merest speck of attraction to a man such as Jess Hadley!

Jeb Tierney hurried into the office, looking behind him at the departing gunfighter.

'What did he want?' was his immediate question, and seeing Lucy's flustered state, asked: 'Are you OK, Lucy? That no-good bastard didn't — '

'No,' she hurriedly assured the farmer. She held out Lane's advertisement. 'Lane wants this printed in tomorrow's *Gazette*.'

Jeb Tierney's eyes flashed over the advertisement.

'You're not going to print it, are you?' he enquired.

'You know, Jeb. Maybe the railroad wouldn't be such a bad thing for the town after all.' Stunned, Tierney was speechless. 'Well, at least this meeting tomorrow will settle the matter one way or the other. Folk will want a railroad or they won't.'

'This is a family town, Lucy,' Tierney said accusatively. 'A place to rear kids in, and have good neighbours. That would all change with a rail spur. Every two-bit no-good would be on our doorstep in no time at all.'

'But without the railroad, the town will likely die, Jeb. We know from experience that business and commerce follow the track.'

'This town has been, and can continue to be, self-sufficient, Lucy.' He waved Lane's advertisement in the air. 'You can't print this.'

'I'm a newspaper, Jeb. My pa always made sure that all shades of opinion were stated in the *Gazette*, and I can do no less. It's what Ned Galt would have expected,' she stated unequivocally.

'I never thought that you'd be taken in by Lane's smooth-tongue, Lucy.' His voice reeked of bitter disappointment. 'Figured that you were way too smart for that to happen.' He held out Lane's advertisement for her to take. 'But I guess that you're no different to a lot of others in this town, who'll do anything to ingratiate themselves to Lane in the hope that they can fill their pockets.

'If Lane's advertisement goes in the *Gazette*, Lucy, my interview doesn't.'

'Your interview will give a balanced argument, Jeb,' she pleaded. 'It will help folk to decide for themselves.'

'Don't know why Lane is bothering calling a meeting. Seems to me that he's already won his argument.' He paused in the open door. 'Hope you and Jess Hadley will be real cosy, Lucy,' he flung back, bitterly.

'Jess Hadley and me? Talk sense, Jeb.'

'That flush on your cheeks speaks louder than any words could, Lucy,'

Tierney said sadly.

When he left, Lucy Galt sat on the chair behind her desk to ponder on Jeb Tierney's words, which were utter rubbish of course. She could never contemplate having anything to do with a man of Hadley's low class. And yet, now that she thought about it, she would not have objected if he had kissed her.

The self-revelation shocked her. Was that why she was suddenly seeing some merit in Samuel Lane's plans for Wayne Creek? She had a decision to make, but she would not make it yet. She would ride out to a brook a couple of miles outside of town where, in its peace and quiet, she did most of her thinking. It was there she had gone when her pa had been killed — *murdered*, the little voice inside her head reminded her. And she had gone there to pray when her ma got the fever that had killed her. She badly needed to clear her head.

Locking up the office, she went to the livery where her buggy was housed.

Samuel Lane was laughing as Jess Hadley relayed what had happened in the office of the *Gazette*.

'Seems you've got honey on your tongue, Jess,' he said. 'A rare and deadly combination, my friend. A honeyed-tongue and a fast draw.'

'You pay for the best, you get the best, Mr Lane,' Jess Hadley chuckled. 'I think you've got company,' he added, looking beyond to the window through which he saw Jeb Tierney storm across the street and head straight for the alley alongside the saloon from where he could gain direct access to Lane's office via a side door. On seeing Tierney, grim and purposeful, Lane sprang out of his chair to turn the lock on the door. A couple of seconds later, the door was tried.

'Lane!' the sodbuster yelled, his voice vibrant with fury. 'Open the door, or I'm coming through anyway. The choice is yours.'

'Hold it right there, Tierney!'

Lane and Hadley recognized the

voice of Darkie Clark.

'I guess Darkie's trying to regain his worth, eh, Jess,' Lane scoffed.

Hadley grinned. 'Never considered he had any worth to begin with.'

'Lane!' Jeb Tierney bellowed, and the door shook with the fury of his beating fists. 'I'm coming through.'

'Tell me what you want me to do, Mr Lane,' Darkie Clark called out.

'You figure I should let Darkie solve a problem?' Lane asked Jess Hadley.

'I figure that if the sodbuster is a problem, he can be dealt with better than having him shot down in town. Especially when there's that meeting tomorrow night, boss,' Hadley counselled. 'As I understand it, Tierney's a pretty popular hombre around here.

'The vote on the railroad might not go so well, if he's lying in the funeral parlour with a weeping widow hanging round town.'

'Wise counsel,' Lane complimented the gunfighter, and went and opened the door.

The second the door was opened, Jeb Tierney, charging from the opposite side of the alley, shoulder ready to attack the door, shot past Samuel Lane and crashed into Jess Hadley.

'Just as well this is no china shop,' Hadley laughed, steadying Tierney.

Darkie Clark charged in behind Tierney, sixgun cocked and ready to fire.

'Leave him be, Darkie,' Lane said. 'It's Jess's opinion that we should hear what Mr Tierney has to say. Isn't that so, Jess?'

'Surely is,' Hadley confirmed.

Darkie Clark glowered at Hadley, a diamond-bright fury lighting his eyes.

'Seems to me that Hadley's got a whole lot to say for himself, Mr Lane,' he growled. 'And it sure looks like you're doin' a whole lot o' listenin' too.'

'Get out,' Lane ordered Clark. Darkie Clark, obviously stunned that his degree of displacement in the order of things had deteriorated so much in so short a time, took up a pose of obstinancy. Lane turned to Hadley. 'Looks like Mr Clark doesn't want to leave. Throw him out, Jess.'

'You're the boss, Mr Lane,' Hadley said, and closed on Clark.

'Move another inch and I'll blow your damn head off!' Clark ranted, threatening Jess Hadley with his drawn pistol.

With the speed of a mountain cat, Hadley went into a crouch and came up under Clark's guard to land a punch in Clark's belly that rocked him back on his heels. The second haymaker caught him flush on the jaw and sent him reeling backwards. Before he could recover even a smidgen of his composure, Hadley added a third pile-driver on the side of Clark's head that spun him out through the open door and sent him sprawling in the alley. Jess Hadley slammed the office door shut.

Smug as a flea on a dog's rump, Samuel Lane strolled to the chair behind his desk and sat down.

'What do you want, Tierney?' he asked.

Jeb Tierney had difficulty in re-adjusting his vision. He had seen men move fast before, but none as quickly as Jess Hadley.

'Well?' Lane barked impatiently.

'Compensation,' the farmer said.

'Compen — what for?'

'For the barn your Moon Raiders burned down last night, that's what for, Lane.'

Lane chuckled. 'You've been out in the sun too long, Tierney. Get out.' He looked to Hadley who moved forward. 'I don't know a damn thing about any Moon Raiders.'

'You pay them, Lane,' Tierney said. 'Most of them are at the other side of the wall in your saloon.'

Lane shook his head.

'You're talking crazy, Tierney. And I don't have to listen. If you've got proof,' he grinned slyly, 'take it to the marshal.'

'I reckon you've overstayed your welcome, mister,' Jess Hadley said. 'Mr Lane is a busy man. Got no time to listen to horse manure.'

So intense was Jeb Tierney's anger

that he obviously considered going for his gun, and might have, had not Lucy Galt burst in.

'What the hell is this?' Lane exploded. 'This is a private office, Miss Galt.'

Lucy Galt's concern was wholly for Jeb Tierney.

'Are you OK, Jeb?'

'I don't need minding, Miss Galt,' he fumed.

'Well then act like you don't,' Lucy flung back. Her rebuke took the sting from the sodbuster's anger. 'It's getting late. Now why don't you go on home to Martha. She'll be fretting, Jeb.'

'Good advice, I'd say,' Jess Hadley commented.

'Anyone ask for your advice!' Tierney growled.

'Come on, Jeb,' Lucy encouraged. 'Your business is finished here.'

'I'll go,' he told Lane. 'But my business with you is far from finished, Lane.'

Samuel Lane shook his head. 'Loco critter,' he chuckled.

But Jess Hadley could see the

concern behind Lane's casual dismissal of Tierney's promise. When they left, Lane made small talk with Hadley for a while, before saying:

'Your throat must be parched, Jess. Why don't you go and get yourself a drink on the house.'

'I sure could do with a drink,' the gunfighter agreed.

'And, ah . . . ' Hadley paused at the door leading to the saloon, 'tell Darkie Clark I want to see him right away. I want to make it plain to him that one more outburst and he'll be hitting the trail, without pay, too.'

Jess Hadley left, his mood thoughtful.

★ ★ ★

Jeb Tierney left town to return home, still as mad as hell at what he saw as Lucy Galt's treachery, which initially he could find no explanation for, until he recalled how taken by Jess Hadley she had seemed to be when he had called, just after Hadley had left her company at the newspaper office. 'You've got to be thinking crazy,' Tierney told himself. 'Lucy Galt taking a shine to a man of Jess Hadley's low class.'

However, the more he thought about it, the more certain he became that the idea was not as loco as it seemed. Lucy Galt would not be the first woman in the West to throw herself away on a man like Hadley, inexplicable as that was to other folk. He supposed that it had been the way through history, and would continue to be so in the future as well because human behaviour did not change all that much, it was just the times lived in that made it seem so.

* * *

Despite Darkie Clark's stated intent to chuck the Lane outfit, when Jess Hadley informed him that Lane wanted to see him in his private office, a privilege offered to only a few close associates, Clark's vow to quit was quickly set aside in his eagerness to regain his former position as Lane's chief enforcer.

Snide laughter was the order among Darkie Clark's cohorts when the door of Samuel Lane's office closed on a grovelling Clark.

'Lane can go stuff his head in a bucket of horseshit,' one man said, mimicking Clark. Another took up the mockery.

'If Lane thinks I'm goin' to kiss his butt, fellas . . .'

The man did not get a chance to finish his reminder of Darkie Clark's firebrand statement of only moments before, drowned out as it was by boisterous laughter. When the laughter died away, the man whose mimickery was interrupted, turned the attention on Jess Hadley who had, during the mimicry of Darkie Clark's lack of backbone, bellied up to the bar.

'Ain't you worried that Darkie'll get inside you again with the boss, Hadley,' he jibed.

Hadley's look was one of contemptuous dismissal, which brought an indignant reaction from his questioner.

'I asked you a question, Hadley?' he growled.

Jess Hadley picked up his beer and slugged liberally, wiped the froth from his mouth, placed the beer back on the bar, looked again at the man with even greater contempt, thought about answering him, and then decided not to.

'Answer me or use that gun you're supposed to be so fast with,' the man ranted.

The mood in the saloon had quickly gone from festive to fraught, and clear ground was opening up between and around the protagonists. The men of the Lane outfit had the advantage over Jess Hadley, in that they knew and had experienced Scoot Leary's ire before, and did not wish to be drawn into his challenge to Hadley because, should they express their reluctance to back him he would probably kill them, and should they throw in their lot with him,

71

Jess Hadley would likely do the same. It was a no win situation, best avoided.

'Ain't no supposing about it, fella,' Hadley drawled, in the fashion of a man who was not troubled by the gauntlet laid down. 'You go for that Colt on your hip and you'll never reach it.' The gunfighter laughed easily. 'And if that sounds like a promise, it is.'

'I'm no slouch with an iron m'self,' Leary bragged.

'Don't doubt that,' Hadley responded. 'But I'm grease-lightning. Maybe even faster.'

Recognizing a statement of fact as opposed to a boast, Scoot Leary began to sweat, because as Hadley turned from the bar to face him, he saw in him the Grim Reaper come a-calling. Eyes switched from Hadley to Leary, awaiting his reaction. If anyone dropped a pin in the saloon at that moment, its reverberations would be ear-shattering. Everyone knew that Scoot Leary was trying desperately to swallow the chunk of stupidity that had got him looking death in the eye. However, along with his pride, his swallow might not be big enough.

* * *

Across the street in the *Gazette* office, Lucy Galt was trying to come to terms with Jeb Tierney's stormy and hostile departure. Much older than she, her friendship with Tierney had been one of respect more than closeness, and had been a carry-over from Tierney's friendship with her father, born on the day they had arrived in Wayne Creek together many years previously, brought together by a common bond of putting down roots in a town that had more frontier than settled about it. They would often joke of an evening while sharing a smoke and a beer, sometimes moonshine if the Indians had not killed the moonshiner, about how Tierney had come West to start a newspaper, having had ambitions to follow in the illustrious footsteps of the great editors and owners back East, and had ended up a farmer. And how Ned Galt had taken the same route to farm and had ended up owning the *Gazette*.

'Why didn't you both set up a newspaper or a farm together,' Lucy had asked one evening, what to her seemed to be a reasonable question.

Her pa had laughed heartily, and Jeb Tierney's laughter had been every bit as robust.

'Because, young lady,' Ned Galt had explained. 'Ornery critters as we both are, we'd end up killing each other.'

Jeb Tierney had added:

'Friends we can be, Lucy. Partners we'd never be.'

'Be like teasing a stick of dynamite with a match,' Martha Tierney had said, picking up the jist of the conversation as she came from the house.

Lucy had not had the opportunity to speak to her pa before he died, which was within seconds of being run over by the wagon, which Jeb was certain had been spooked by Darkie Clark, but had she had, she was sure that Ned Galt's advice would be the same as he had given her on numerous occasions since her ma had passed on, and that would have been to place her trust in Jeb Tierney and seek his counsel should the need arise. The need had arisen, and instead of acting on her pa's advice, she had distanced Jeb from her by her silly acceptance of Samuel Lane's advertisement for insertion in the *Gazette*. But what choice had she? By refusing Lane's right to be heard, and using the newspaper to promote Tierney's opinion exclusively, she would have betrayed Ned Galt's rigid adherance to giving voice to all shades of opinion.

'Democracy, girl,' he had once said, when she had asked him about the inclusion in the newspaper of a denunciation of the *Gazette*'s editorial stand against a politician whose doctrine was, as Galt had seen it, a danger to the very democracy he had fought for, but on the surface had the veneer of wisdom to it. 'The *Gazette* has a duty to let every man be heard, so that the people can decide for themselves.'

Maybe, she thought guiltily, if she had taken the time to explain to Jeb Tierney, rather than simply getting on her high horse, spouting her rights in this and her rights in that, she could have persuaded him of Ned Galt's principles which, at her pa's graveside, she had vowed to live up to and thereby have retained Jeb's friendship at a time when she was certain that she would need it.

It was tough having to admit to herself that she had been unduly influenced by Jess Hadley's visit, but that was exactly what had happened. How could she possibly have traded Jeb Tierney's friendship for a couple of breathless moments of Hadley's company?

★　★　★

'Tell you what, mister,' Jess Hadley told Scoot Leary, 'why don't I just finish my beer and put all of this down to ill judgement?'

Scoot Leary wished that he could accept Jess Hadley's offer, unusually generous as it was, coming from a man who, any day, would rather enjoy the pleasure of killing a man than back-off. But he knew that if he did as Hadley had suggested, he'd be finished in this town and a hundred more up the line. Because nothing travelled faster in the West than the story of a man's yellow streak.

'You might even join me,' Hadley said, his offer causing slack jawed consternation in the saloon. 'I've tasted beer that was a whole lot better in my time, but . . . ' He shrugged. 'A man's got to make do with what's on offer, I guess.'

'I'd rather kiss a mule's behind, than drink with you, Hadley,' Leary barked.

'You are a mule's behind,' the gunfighter said, 'thinking you stand a chance of beating me to the draw.'

'Only one way to find out,' Leary

croaked, his voice reedy with anxiety.

Jess Hadley shrugged. 'If this is the way you want to die, friend. You call it.'

'I don't want no favours,' Leary spat.

* * *

In his office, Samuel Lane had been listening to the lengthening silence from the saloon, while he outlined to Darkie Clark the task he was setting him.

'Gone kind of quiet out there, ain't it?' he said.

So pleased was Darkie Clark to be back in Lane's favour, all he could hear was the sound of his own voice as he gladly accepted the assignment his boss had handed him, promising:

'I won't let you down, Mr Lane. Of that you can be certain.'

However, increasingly intrigued by the stillness from the watering-hole at the other side of the thin partition, Lane was not interested in Clark's buttkissing.

'Go see what's happening out there,' he ordered his lackey.

'Sure, Mr Lane,' Darkie Clark said, miffed at Lane's lack of interest in his reassurance.

Clark went to the door that opened to the saloon.

* * *

Lucy Galt had made up her mind to try and mend fences with Jeb Tierney and was on her way to the livery to hire a horse. The rig she usually drove would slow her up. By the time she caught up with the farmer he would have reached the rocky terrain bordering his farm, so a horse would be much more practical, though infinitely more uncomfortable. And she was not a great rider to boot. Hers had been the upbringing of a lady. Ned Galt never figured on her losing both parents, the expectation being that he would live into ripe old age.

'I reckon Alice would be about right for you, Miss Galt,' the livery keeper opined, saddling a mare. 'Got a real sweet nature, has Alice, and knows the territory better than most men. Just sweet talk her and she'll find her own way.'

Mounted, Lucy rode out of town, the object of much curiosity from a couple of Lane hardcases leaning on the saloon's batwings. One immediately vanished back into the saloon, no doubt to report her departure to Lane, who liked to be kept informed of the movement of anyone in town who might hinder the fulfilment of his ambitions.

Riding past, Lucy struck a devil may care pose.

★　★　★

Scoot Leary was on the verge of drawing when Darkie Clark opened the office door.

'Mr Lane wants to know what's goin' on?' he demanded.

'I'm just about to kill this fella,' Hadley said.

Darkie Clark's jaw dropped.

'Well?' Lane called out. 'What's going on, Darkie?'

Overcoming his perplexion, Clark said: 'Scoot Leary's got himself in a tangle with Hadley, boss. Looks like Scoot is on his way to hell, if you ask me.'

A moment later, Samuel Lane appeared in the open door, his eyes flashing between Leary and Hadley. 'What's this all about?' His question was addressed to Jess Hadley.

'Asked him a question, Mr Lane,' Leary said. 'Hadley smart-mouthed me. So I figure — '

'Clear out!' Lane roared.

'Clear out?' Scoot Leary asked, stunned.

'You heard me,' Lane bellowed. 'Dunderheads like you I can get for a penny a dozen. Men of Jesse's calibre aren't as easy to find. And I don't want a toerag like you around upsetting him.'

'That a fact!' Leary yelled. He went for his gun, but Darkie Clark, anticipating Leary's move and mood, already had his gun out and blasting. Scoot

Leary was lifted clean off his feet and pitched across the saloon, dead before he hit the ground.

'Thanks, Darkie,' Lane said. His attention then focused on Jess Hadley. 'I didn't see you stepping in to save my hide from that mad dog killer, Hadley?'

'I reckoned my assistance wasn't needed, Mr Lane. I figured that Darkie was well capable of taking care of Leary.'

'Yeah,' Clark bragged. 'And that goes for any man in this outfit.' He settled his gaze on Jess Hadley. 'You too, mister.'

'I ain't arguing, Darkie,' Jess Hadley said in a friendly manner.

Samuel Lane slung an arm round Darkie Clark's shoulders. 'You run along now on that errand I set you, Darkie.'

'Sure thing, boss.'

Clark swaggered out of the saloon.

'You men,' Lane pointed. 'Sling the trash out.'

The indicated men picked up Scoot Leary's body.

'Where do we take him, Mr Lane? The funeral parlour?'

'Funeral parlour!' Lane scoffed. 'Just dig a hole and sling him in it.'

Lane went back into his office and slammed the door shut. Leary removed, the saloon settled back to business as usual. Hadley delayed for a couple of minutes before drifting out of the saloon.

6

Once his temper cooled, Jeb Tierney slowed his pace and rode more leisurely. Of late his frustration with Samuel's Lane's unchallenged march to dominance over town and valley, with more and more either moving on or yielding to his will, had made him tetchy; a tetchiness which he had unfairly off-loaded on Martha, who, of all people, did not deserve to suffer the barbs of his anger. He sometimes thought, and more so of late, that by marrying Martha he had blighted her life. Maybe he was wrong, but he had reached the conclusion that had she tied the knot with Ned Galt instead, she would have had a life and a man more in tune with her expectations. Often, in the night, he would lie awake and wonder what Martha was dreaming of, or rather who she was dreaming of.

Several times he had seen her smile in her sleep, her face lighting up the way it never did when she was awake and he was around, and he reckoned that at that time she was dreaming of Ned Galt. Because her smile then, had been an exact replica of how she had smiled when she had first met Galt. Those times she had shed most if not all of the weight she carried on her shoulders, and when Ned Galt had been alive she would look at him and Jeb knew that she was having the same thought as he was, and that was that, like Martha having married the wrong man, Ned Galt, too, had married the wrong woman.

'Maybe we should accept Lane's offer, Jeb,' Martha had said, only the previous week. 'Move on. Make a fresh start.'

'No,' he had resolutely refused. 'I won't be run out, Martha!'

'Lane's price is as close to fair as you'll get, Jeb,' she had argued in her quiet way.

'It's not the money,' he had countered. 'It's the principle, Martha.'

'Sometimes you just have to let go, Jeb,' had been her opinion. 'Any man can only fight for so long.'

'Where would we go if we left here?'

'Does it matter, if we'll be happy, Jeb?'

'That's woman talk,' he had blustered, in the absence of an argument that would come near to making sense.

Now as he rode along, Jeb Tierney began to think that, after all, there might be something in what Martha had said. Maybe he should swing round and ride back to town and accept Samuel Lane's offer? There would be other valleys. Other towns. Maybe he could start a general store? Or maybe a livery? Or maybe that newspaper he had intended setting up when he had arrived in Wayne Creek.

He had drifted into farming, but had grown to love the scent of ploughed earth and fresh crops. At first he had been resentful of Ned Galt beating him to the punch to set up the *Gazette*, but later, as farming got into his blood, he would not have swapped places.

Hell, he'd talk to Martha when he got home; talk to her in a way he had not spoken before. Preoccupied as he was, his horse stumbled and he barely stayed in the saddle as it lurched forward. Had the mare not stumbled, the bullet that spun off the rockface close by would have killed him.

He leaped out of the saddle and scrambled for cover in nearby boulders, chased by the bushwhacker's lead, buzzing round him like a hive of angry bees. As he crouched in the boulders, Tierney knew that he was alive by sheer luck, because whoever the shooter was had an expertise with the weapon that had been gained from long practise. That he could tell by the angle of the bullets, he was safe in hiding, because to nail him the shooter would have to climb to a higher point in the canyon, and that would leave him exposed to return fire, albeit from a sixgun, with which Tierney would need the devil's own luck to score a hit. However, he guessed that right now the bush-whacker, having seen his target's miraculous escape, might not be of a mind to take even the small risk that climbing higher up would entail. So how would the stand-off be resolved? Night was closing in fast, and the bushwhacker would be aware of how easy it would be for his intended victim to slip away in the shadowy dusk.

In his lair, Darkie Clark was thinking just that, and knew that if he did not successfully carry out the murderous task which Samuel Lane had assigned him, he would be finished in these parts, and just when it looked like Lane's plans were about to yield a pot of gold from which he hoped to scoop a share.

While he was tussling with his dilemma, with depressingly little hope of finding a solution without risk to his hide, an answer appeared in the shape of Lucy Galt riding anxiously into the canyon. Spotting Jeb Tierney's loose horse she called out:

'Jeb. It's Lucy Galt. Can you hear me, Jeb?'

There was apprehension in her voice.

'Get outta here, Lucy,' Tierney called back. 'Fast!'

But it was already too late. A bullet buzzed close to Lucy.

'Stay right where you are, Miss Galt!'

Jeb recognized the voice of Darkie Clark.

'Leave her be, Clark,' Tierney shouted. 'It's me you want.'

The second he had spoken the gunslinger's name, Jeb knew that he had made an error. He had foolishly established the killer's identity, and now that it was known, Darkie Clark had to make certain that no one lived to reveal it.

'Stand up, where I can see you, Tierney!' Clark shouted angrily.

'Don't, Jeb,' Lucy called out. 'Clark will kill you.'

The darkening canyon echoed Darkie

Clark's laughter ghostily.

'Tell you what, Tierney,' he said. 'If you don't show yourself right now, I'll drop the woman.'

'He'll kill me anyway,' Lucy said. 'He can't afford to leave a breathing witness to murder. But if you stay put, he'll have to flush you out, Jeb. That will give you the chance to avenge my death, if that's the way it's to be.'

'Clark!' Tierney hailed. 'There is another way. If you walk away from this, me and Lucy will forget you were ever here.'

'What kind of a fool do you think I am,' the gunslinger returned.

'What have you got to worry about anyway,' Tierney reminded Clark. 'The marshal is on Lane's payroll.'

'And what's to stop you riding to the next town and summoning a US marshal, Tierney?'

'My word is worth something to me, Clark.'

'Yeah? Well it ain't worth tiddly to me, Tierney!'

Befuddled, Darkie Clark sat on the hard ground and found an unexpected solution to his dilemma. He shovelled the soft earth with his hands and his eyes glowed at what the short stub of metal sticking out of the ground was — a rifle, rusted and busted, but none the less valuable, because a thought had come to mind that would, he reckoned, have him strutting back to town like a damn peacock.

'Tierney! he hollered. 'You listening?'

'I'm listening,' came Tierney's response.

'Look,' Darkie Clark drawled, 'I've been thinking. Maybe this idea of yours about we all going our separate ways and keeping our mouths shut might just work dandy.'

Jeb Tierney was instantly alert.

'Yeah,' he encouraged. 'I guess it will.'

'Now, I'm trusting you, Tierney,' Clark said. 'I'm going to stand up where you can see me. Then I'll toss my rifle down, as a gesture of good faith. Then you and the woman can ride out of here. You'll be under no threat from a sixgun from this range.

'Agreed?'

Tierney did not trust Darkie Clark for a second, but right now he could not fathom out the gunslinger's scheme, but a scheme there was, of that he was certain. All he could hope for was that whatever Clark was planning, he'd spot it in time to counter his treachery.

'Agreed, Tierney?' Clark checked.

'Agreed,' Tierney called back.

'Standing up now,' Clark shouted.

Tierney watched as closely as he could in the gathering gloom for any sign of devilry by Clark. But to his surprise, the hardcase stood up holding his rifle above his head. 'Here goes,' he said, and tossed the rifle down into the canyon. 'Good as my word, Tierney. You and Miss Galt are free to leave. But remember, not a word of this.'

'I'll keep my word, Clark,' Tierney promised.

'Me, too,' Lucy added, relieved that the dangerous impasse had been resolved.

What was Clark up to? He surely was up to something, Tierney reckoned. But what could he possibly do without a rifle?

'Be seeing you folk back in town,' Clark said, his tone friendly.

Tierney came from cover and walked cautiously to where his horse was, never taking an eye off Darkie Clark. He mounted up and joined Lucy Galt.

'This is surely a miracle, Jeb,' she said. 'I thought we were done for.'

'And I can't believe we're not,' Tierney said.

'You take care now,' Clark called, as they rode away, and then bent down to pick up his Winchester, grinning wolfishly. 'Idiots,' he snorted, and raised the rifle to get Tierney in its sights. On hearing his name whispered, Clark spun round.

'Drop the rifle!' the unexpected visitor commanded.

His surprise overcome, Clark roared: 'Damn you!' He levelled his rifle to fire.

A sixgun exploded in the gloom.

Darkie Clark's final scream filled every inch of the terrain, as he spun off his high perch and plunged into the canyon, bouncing like a straw doll off the rocks, his rifle clattering down with him.

'That cur fooled us,' Lucy Galt said. Jeb Tierney scanned the top of the canyon but saw no one. 'Who was that, Jeb?'

'Now wouldn't that be good to know, Lucy,' he replied.

7

On hearing the clomp of hoofs, Martha Tierney leaped off the chair she was sitting in, a chair from which she had hardly moved since that morning when Jess Hadley had left, worried as she was about Jeb's safety and the possibility of facing widowhood, convinced as she had become on recalling where she had heard the name Jess Hadley before and also that gent's profession. He had admitted that he was on his way into town to see Samuel Lane, and his and Jeb's arrival would not be far apart. She was hurrying to the table to quench the lamp when the voice she heard hailing the house made her heart sing out in a way that she had never thought it would.

'Martha, it's me!'

Martha rushed to open the cabin door. She had so often regretted not having married Ned Galt instead of Jeb Tierney, but the recent troubles in the valley had had her fretting about the loss of Jeb in a way she had never imagined she would have. And today she had felt the possible loss of her husband more keenly than she would have thought even a short time ago. Hard times and no offspring had driven a wedge between her and Jeb, and the more she worried about the issue, the more troubled she had become.

'Maybe if you could relax a little, Martha,' Saul Brannigan, the Wayne Creek doctor had told her. 'Worry and fretting are known to, if not hinder conception, certainly not help any.'

Lord, how she had tried to heed the good doctor's advice, but there never seemed to be any time in which she could be easy, with trouble being heaped on trouble. The previous year a long dry spell had yielded up crops that weeds had more consistency and strength than. Then Lane arrived in town and soon after the Moon Raiders had put in an appearance. But now the new barn which Jeb had worked so hard to build was a charred ruin, as were the crops he had stored in it. Mortgage payments were way overdue, and with near empty coffers foreclosure would be a real possibility.

But they were all worries for the future. Right now Jeb was home safe and that was all in the world that mattered to Martha Tierney. She yanked open the cabin door and rushed outside to greet him, fright halting her steps briefly before she recognized the rider with Jeb. Martha's gaze went beyond her husband to the form slung over the saddle of the horse he had in tow.

'It's a long story best told on a full belly, Martha,' he said, following her gaze. Lucy's come to stay over.' As he dismounted Martha rushed into his arms, clinging to him with a fierceness she had not displayed since those heady months after marriage when the world seemed full of hope and promise.

'Thank God you're home safe, Jeb,' Martha wept, but her tears were tears of joy and happiness. 'Did you see Jess Hadley in town?'

Tierney tensed.

'How did you know Jess Hadley was in this neck of the woods, Martha,' he questioned her anxiously, standing her back from him to look at her for any signs of injury or worse.

'He stopped by this morning on his way into town, shortly after you left, Jeb. Wanted to fill his canteen. I told him to keep riding.'

'And he did?' Jeb quizzed.

'Yes. There was no danger. I had him covered with a rifle.'

'But you can't shoot straight, Martha.'

She laughed joyously. 'He didn't know that, Jeb.'

He laughed along with her, while Lucy Galt kept her distance, not wanting to intrude on the tender moment Jeb and Martha Tierney were sharing. She knew that their relationship had become rocky in recent times, but now those times seemed to be behind them.

'It ain't like a killer of Jess Hadley's poison to simply ride away,' Jeb said, ponderingly. 'Don't you think that's strange, Lucy?'

'It is,' she agreed.

'I must have scared him, I guess,' Martha said cockily.

'Jess Hadley's not the kind of hombre to scare that easy,' Jeb Tierney mumured, his thoughts even deeper. He shook his head. 'Makes no sense,' he concluded.

'All that matters now is that you're home, Jeb,' Martha said, brushing away her tears.

Jeb drew her fondly into his arms.

'Maybe I should go to town to wrangle with Lane more often.'

'You stay far away from town and right here with me from now on, Jeb Tierney,' Martha playfully scolded him.

'I've got to deliver back Darkie Clark's body, Martha.'

'Darkie Clark?' Martha looked to the man draped across the saddle of the horse in tow.

'Tried to bushwhack Lucy and me,' Jeb said.

'Killing Clark will bring big trouble,' Martha fretted. 'Not that he didn't deserve killing.'

'I didn't kill him, Martha.'

'But if you didn't, who did?'

'That's the mystery, honey,' Tierney said.

'Don't you go to town, Jeb,' Martha pleaded. 'I'll ride in and tell the marshal that Darkie Clark's body is here, waiting to be collected. He can come himself or send the undertaker. Now,' her mood which had become solemn on hearing of Darkie Clark's demise and the fears that his death raised in her for Jeb's safety, lifted, 'you two come inside the house and I'll prepare supper.'

Jeb Tierney followed, more happy than he had been for a long time. And determined, now that relations between him and Martha had thawed, to make damn sure that their future together would fulfil the bright promise of their wedding day.

Had he gone to the window to look out, he would have seen a dark horseman on the hill overlooking the cabin turn and ride away, satisfied that they had reached home safely.

8

Samuel Lane was pacing his office, wondering what was keeping his assassin Darkie Clark. He was not yet ready to think about Clark failing to kill Tierney, and sought other explanations for his non-appearance which, troubling, were not coming to mind. Clark was an efficient and merciless killer who had a proficiency with rifle, sixgun and knife. He had also, in his time, strangled a couple of enemies. In fact he was not far short of Jess Hadley in ability and meanness. However, Hadley had a slight edge, and it was that edge that might make all the difference in the end. Maybe, he considered, that he should have handed the job of offing the troublesome sodbuster to Hadley, but he reckoned that it was wisest to keep both men relatively happy to get the best out of both. Because either, if riled, could be bad medicine.

There was a knock on the door.

'That you, Darkie?' he hailed.

Jess Hadley entered.

'Darkie ain't around, Mr Lane.'

'I know he isn't!' Lane barked.

'I've been wondering where he might have got to?'

'Why would you wonder, Hadley? You're not paid to worry.'

'If you don't mind my saying so,' Hadley said, 'you look kind of worried yourself, Mr Lane.'

Lane slumped wearily into the chair behind his desk. 'To tell you the truth, Jess, I am.'

'What's the problem?'

'It's Darkie Clark. I sent him after that bastard Tierney to . . . '

'Kill him?' the gunfighter said, when Lane became suddenly reticent. 'When?'

'A couple of hours ago.'

'Should be back long before now, unless Clark is going to talk Tierney to death.'

'I know Darkie should be back long

before now!' Lane barked. 'That he's not is what's worrying me.'

'You're not thinking that Tierney might have . . . ?'

'Every man gets lucky some time,' Lane muttered.

'Tierney would be easy meat for Darkie Clark, boss,' he reassured Samuel Lane.

'Like I said,' Lane growled. 'Maybe Tierney got lucky.'

'Well, I guess he might have at that, Mr Lane.'

Samuel Lane studied the gunfighter. 'Sounds like you're talking from experience, Jess?'

'Surely am, Mr Lane. There was this fella, Crow — Jack Crow, a US marshal. He was on my tail and I shouldn't have dallied in a town down near the border, but I got into a hot poker game and into an even hotter dove.'

He grinned in the winning way he had.

'A man's got to have his pleasures.'

Lane snorted. 'I'm partial to a little pleasure myself, Jess.'

'Anyway,' the gunfighter continued, 'this fella Crow showed up. I wasn't unduly worried. I heard tell that he was fast with a gun, but I wasn't counting on him being faster than me.' Jess Hadley snorted. 'I reckoned that no-one was faster than me. And that's what very nearly made me a harp-player, I can tell you.'

'This fella Crow was faster?' Lane asked, gripped by Hadley's story.

'Grease lightning fast,' Hadley confirmed.

'So how come — ?'

'I'm still around? Well, it was a real cloudy day when Crow called me out. But just as Crow drew, the cloud broke and the noon sun shone full blast on the window of the general store and dazzled Crow for the second I needed to nail him.

'Sometimes a man's luck goes bad. You reckon Darkie's went bad?'

Lane shrugged, his concern for Clark

taking second place to his interest in Jess Hadley's story. 'I thought you were the fastest around, Hadley?' he grunted.

'No matter how fast you are, there's always someone faster, Mr Lane, and that's a fact. All a fella can do is hope that his path won't cross with this faster draw, and that he'll die in bed of old age slugging from a bottle of whiskey and in the company of an accomodating woman.'

He chuckled.

'Better still if this woman's caused him to die with her antics.'

'Never heard of a hombre called Jack Crow?' Lane said sourly, in no mood for banter.

'Well, now you have, boss. Now about Darkie Clark, anything you want me to do?'

'Not much you can do. Come morning, if he hasn't shown up, ride out to Tierney's place and find out what's happened.'

'I figure if you'd handed me the job, it would be done by now,' Hadley said.

Lane shifted uneasily in his chair.

'Well, if Clark hasn't done the job, it's yours. OK?'

Jess Hadley stretched and yawned.

'I've kind of got this hankering for a good killing right now,' he sighed.

'You'll get busy real soon, if people around here don't come round to my point of view, Jess,' Lane growled.

'That's the way I like it, Mr Lane. Lots of lead in the air.' He laughed. 'Nothing as soothing to the lungs as the acrid smell of gunsmoke, I say.'

'Meantime, there's this rancher called Blanchard. He's getting what I'd call a *Tierney streak*. Could be trouble. I think it's time he had a visit from the Moon Raiders.'

'The Moon Raiders, boss?'

'Yeah.' Lane chuckled. 'An idea I got a while back. Worked good, too. I think it's about time you started to earn those dollars I'll be stuffing your pockets with, Jess.'

★　★　★

'That was a delicious meal, Martha,' Lucy Galt complimented her host. 'Like the ones my ma used to serve up.' There was a sadness in Lucy's voice.

They were alone, Jeb having, against Martha's pleading, ridden back to town to inform its rotten marshal about Darkie Clark's demise.

Lucy had added her protest to Martha Tierney's.

'Martha is right, Jeb. Town will be no place to be when Samuel Lane hears about the death of Darkie Clark. Clark was a lynchpin in his plans.'

'Not anymore,' Tierney stated. 'Clark's been the second string since Jess Hadley showed up.'

'That's a thought,' Lucy murmured.

'What is?' Tierney questioned.

'Why Lane didn't send Hadley to do his dirty work. I mean if, as you say, Jeb, that Clark has been displaced by Hadley.'

'That's easy to figure,' the farmer pronounced. 'Lane will want no one's nose out of joint when he's about to reap the riches he'd been aiming for. So, I figure that by sending Darkie Clark on a killer's errand, he was counting on keeping Clark on side.'

'Makes sense,' was Lucy Galt's conclusion.

'On my way back from town, I'll swing by Luke Blanchard's place,' Jeb told Martha, 'jaw about happenings in the valley and Lane's malignant influence in the town and its hinterland. I reckon if anyone will stand with me against Lane, it'll be Luke.'

Before taking his leave, Martha again pleaded with him to stay home.

'I've got to deliver Darkie Clark's body, Martha,' he said, a little exasperated by her repeated attempts to change his mind. But, thinking of Martha's fulsome welcome home, he quickly curtailed his annoyance and spoke kindly: 'Even Clark deserves a decent burial.'

'If you ask me, you should have left him right where he was!' Martha snapped. 'And Samuel Lane won't go to the bother of burying Clark,' Martha opined.

'For me to do nothing about trying to get Clark treated decently, would make me no better than him or Lane, I reckon,' Jeb said.

'You're right, of course, honey,' Martha Tierney agreed, the rancour leaving her voice. 'I married a good man in you, Jeb Tierney. And I don't want to lose you. Don't you understand that?'

She kissed him full on the lips, much to Tierney's embarrassment.

'We've got a guest,' he scolded Martha.

'I ain't doing anything I shouldn't be doing, Jeb.'

'And what the heck are you grinning from ear to ear about, Miss Galt?' Tierney asked. And when Martha kissed him again, 'Darn it woman,' Jeb exclaimed, gently distancing himself from Martha. 'Ain't you had enough to eat.'

Lucy Galt's smile became an explosive laugh in which Martha Tierney whole-heartedly joined her, as Jeb left, as red-faced as a first time kissed youngster. When he walked into the door, having, in his confusion forgotten to open it, the women's laughter reached new heights that followed him right across the yard to where his horse was hitched.

When their laughter faded, the reflective sadness which had, moments before descended on Lucy Galt, returned.

'You miss her a lot, don't you, Lucy?' Martha said. 'Your ma.'

'More and more every day, Martha.'

'More than Ned?'

'Oh, I miss my pa as well. But I think Pa's real child was the *Gazette*. The times I heard him talk about anything else could be counted on one hand. Ma would sit and listen, the very essence of patience. I often wondered why she just didn't tell him to shut up while she had her say. And a time or two I told her so, she scolded me. Told me that I should be listening and learning every chance I got, because one day I would be the owner of the *Gazette*, and Pa would expect nothing less of me than the commitment he had to the newspaper.

''Honest newsprint is what democracy is built on,' she would say, mimicking Pa's gruff as gravel voice. 'And that's what will keep this great nation free of the malign philosophies and doctrines that would steal freedom of speech from us.''

Lucy Galt's sigh was long and weary and far beyond her years.

'And you know, Martha. I'm beginning to doubt if I can be as zealous as Pa would have wanted me to be. I'm not even sure if owning and editing a newspaper is a proper job for a woman.

'Sometimes it seems to me that Pa's policy of giving every man his say, good bad or indifferent, doesn't serve the cause of right. I mean, does a man like Samuel Lane deserve the same rights as another, more upright man?'

'I'd say not,' Martha Tierney said. 'But . . . ' she took Lucy's hands in hers. 'I don't own a newspaper, so I can hold that view without it doing much harm to anyone. On the other hand, as a newspaper proprietor, it's your duty to set aside your own opinions and feelings, Lucy.

'Ned Galt was right. Honest newsprint is what will protect our freedom of speech and person. But the price we have to pay for that democracy, like when we have to let opposing forces have their say, is sometimes hard to swallow.'

Lucy laughed gently.

'You know, Martha,' she said softly. 'You and my Pa would have been peas in a pod.'

Martha Tierney might just a short time ago, have had her regrets and doubts about not having married Ned Galt when he had proposed to her, but not now. The possibility that Jeb might have died in town that day, and her discovery of how much she would have missed him, had cleared her mind of any thought other than being a good wife to Jeb Tierney. She had come to realize, albeit late, that she had married a good man in Jeb, and she was determined now to make up for the time she had spent dreaming about what it would have been like to be Mrs Ned Galt.

'More apple pie, Lucy?'

'I'm stuffed, Martha.'

They sat by the fire, each woman with her own thoughts.

9

Conscious of the dangers of night-riding for beast and man, Jeb Tierney set a cautious pace for town, constantly checking for any sign of trouble. Samuel Lane would have long ago been worried about Darkie Clark not having put in an appearance back in town, and might have sent searchers, not out of any concern for Clark, but by way of tying up any loose ends that might be unravelling. The moon was full, and its light was a blessing that could also be a curse. It might mean that Lane's Moon Raiders would be on the prowl. The route through the canyon where Clark had ambushed him, was the shortest one to town, but Tierney gave it a wide berth, because if Lane had dispatched men to discover why Darkie Clark had not returned from his killer's errand, he could cross paths with them in the canyon if Clark had made known to his employer the location for his foul deed of cold-blooded murder.

As he rode along, Jeb Tierney began to wonder about who had shot Darkie Clark? And why he had not shown himself to take credit for his actions? It was a mystery that occupied him all the way to town.

Frank Jackson, the marshal of Wayne Creek was to be found most nights in the Bucking Buffalo saloon as Samuel Lane's guest, and tonight was no exception, Jeb Tierney being just in time to catch the crooked lawman as he was about to leave the marshal's office to enjoy Lane's largesse, obviously taken aback on seeing Jeb Tierney. 'You, Tierney,' he snorted, a bad-tempered scowl on his face. 'Thought you sodbusters went to bed early. So what d'ya want?'

'I've come to inform you about an ambush, and to deliver up the bush-whacker's body, Marshal.'

Jackson's interest was instantly keen and edgy.

'Ambush? Bushwhacker's body?' he said neutrally, though Tierney was in no doubt that Lane's lackey was fully aware of Darkie Clark's mission. 'What're you talking about, Tierney?'

'I'm sure Lane has shared his concern with you about Darkie Clark's disappearance, Marshal,' Tierney scoffed, 'and his treacherous assignment, too. Thought you were looking at a ghost just now, I reckon. Well, I guess you'd never expect that I'd stand a chance against Clark.'

For the time being, Tierney decided to keep the involvement of the mysterious terminator to himself. In time he would give him full credit, but right now it might shake up Lane if he thought that he had the skill and wit to get the upper hand in a tussle with Darkie Clark. In the West, and with a man like Samuel Lane, reputation was everything.

'Now, Tierney,' Jackson said, trying

to smile a carefree smile but failing, 'why would Mr Lane tell *me* about anything like that, seeing that I'm the law in this town?'

'Law!' Jeb Tierney mocked. 'You're a Lane bootlicker, Jackson. Clark's horse is hitched to the rail outside. He's across the saddle.' Tierney turned to leave. 'I'll leave it to you to tell your friend Lane, Marshal.'

'Not so fast, Tierney!' The rotten lawman was out of his chair, sixgun cocked. 'If, as you say, Darkie Clark is dead, there'll be questions to answer. As the law in this town, I just can't take your side of this yarn as gospel. There'll have to be an investigation to fix blame where it rightly should be fixed. And until that's done, you're staying right here in a cell.'

Jackson was slapping himself on the back, figuring that he had extricated himself from a tricky problem with aplomb.

Jeb thought about telling Jackson that Lucy Galt could verify his story, but he kept quiet for fear of putting Lucy in danger.

'Take one step towards that door, and I'll drop you, Tierney,' Jackson warned, his trigger finger itching. Jeb Tierney turned slowly. The marshal gestured towards the cells with his pistol. 'You're goin' to be my guest 'til all this is sorted out.'

He sneered.

'Then I'll hang you!' His laughter was mocking. 'After a fair trial, of course.'

Tierney was furious with himself. He had not, more fool he, anticipated the marshal's move, and cursed that he had been so stupid as to think that Jackson would not act to protect his benefactor Samuel Lane.

'Real convenient that you dropped by, Tierney,' Jackson crowed. 'I think I can persuade Mr Lane to give us the use of his saloon as a courtroom tomorrow. You should be swingin' in the breeze by noon, I reckon.

'I knew that stout oak at the south

end of Main would have its use some day. Of course, we should hang you on a proper gallows, but why put the town to the expense. Now pick a cell and git inside! Unless you'd prefer to dispense with a hangin', and I drop you right on the spot you're standin' on. All the same to me.'

Tierney's fury with himself sharpened considerably. He should have let Clark rot in that canyon, instead of being full of dumb principles and grandiose ideas about the right thing to do. But he would sure as hell not step inside a cell. However, shoulders slumped, he pretended to comply with Jackson's order. Passing a chair, he grabbed it and slung it at the marshal. Ducking the flying chair sent Jackson's aim askew, and his bullet whizzed harmlessly past Tierney to shatter the wall clock behind the desk. He lunged at the rotten lawman and they went down in a heap kicking and punching. Being the fitter and more hard-muscled of the pair, Jackson having been workshy for years, Jeb Tierney's fists were swifter and his punches harder and more punishing.

From the street, distant yet, footsteps pounded on the boardwalk. Any second now Lane's cohorts would come crashing in the door to investigate the gunfire from the marshal's office. Tierney knew that he had only seconds to finish Jackson off and make his escape. Drawing a fist up from the floor he landed the haymaker on the marshal's chin and drove him across the room arms and legs flaying, at the end of which he stood stock still for a second, groaned, and then hit the floor face first.

Tierney swiftly dragged him to the door and used Jackson's deadweight as a door stop to slow up the Lane bunch. Then, moving with the swiftness of a mountain cat, he made his way to the back door and let himself out into the backlot behind the jail, from where he quickly made his way along the alley at the side of the jail, edging up slowly to the opening on to Main. Four men, with at least a dozen in back up, were heaving against the law office door to gain entry. Luckily for him, Tierney had hitched his horse to the rail outside the general store rather than at the marshal's office. He now made tracks for the mare, praying that the horse would not neigh or snicker on seeing him, as she sometimes did. Just as he was about to vault into the saddle, one of the men outside the marshal's office glanced along the street and hollered:

'It's Tierney. He's getting away!'

All effort to gain entrance to the law office was abandoned. Guns began blasting. The air round Tierney as he rode low in the saddle out of town buzzed with flying lead. Up ahead more men were running from the saloon, slinging more lead at him. It was a miracle he was still in the saddle, but he feared that he would not be for long more.

10

Jeb Tierney veered left and charged along an alley near the blacksmith's, which he used as a dumping ground now that the backlot behind his workshop had no more room left. No man in his sane senses used the alley by day, let alone at night. And though the moon lit the alley, it was no help at all, casting eerie and confusing shadows, making it difficult for the hard riding farmer to distinguish quickly between shadow and substance in a place where a mistake could see him impaled on the shaft of a discarded wagon or a busted plough, and a hundred and one other equally deadly obstacles.

'Cut him off at the north end of Main,' a voice that he recognized as Samuel Lane's shouted. 'He has to swing that way, because he can't get through the smithie's backlot.'

Tierney was forced into a full gallop, with all the dangers that brought. But somehow, by God's good grace only, he reckoned, he cleared the backlots and cut back onto the main drag ahead of Lane's army of running men giving pursuit, guns bucking.

Back on the porch of the saloon, finding himself alone, Samuel Lane had an idea that would put the final nail in the troublesome Jeb Tierney's coffin. Checking the street to make sure that no-one was watching, he hurried across the street to the rear of the jail and let himself in by the unlocked back door and appeared in the marshal's office just as Frank Jackson was getting groggily to his feet, massaging a dislocated jaw.

'Mr Lane,' he said, surprised at Lane's unorthrodox entry.

'Just came to check on your welfare, Frank,' Lane said smoothly, coming closer.

'Did you get that bastard Tierney?' the marshal asked, his wits suddenly coming together.

'Don't you worry.' Lane came closer still. 'The boys will nail him.'

'I won't wait until tomorrow to hang him. I'll do it right now!'

'Hang him?' Lane enquired, knowing the reason for the statement, having seen Darkie Clark's body draped across his horse.

Jackson filled Lane in on what had started all the commotion.

Samuel Lane was now toe to toe with Jackson. 'That sure was a jaw-buster Tierney laid on you,' he sympathised. 'Better let the doc have a look at it, Frank,' he added pretending to examine the marshal's crooked jaw.

'Tierney's goin' to hang slow,' Jackson vowed, again massaging his swollen jaw.

'Pity you won't be around to see it,' Lane said, barely above a whisper.

'Huh? Of course I'll be . . . ' Marshal Frank Jackson's eyes popped wide and filled with pain, as the knife which had appeared as if by magic in Lane's right hand, was driven into his gut, twisted and driven deeper still.

Jackson whimpered and slid to the ground, clutching at Lane, who sneeringly shoved him away.

'I'll make sure that Tierney swings for *your* murder, Frank,' he mocked the dying lawman. He stepped over the marshal's body and left the way he had entered.

'Tierney got away, Mr Lane,' one of the men reported to Lane as he crossed the street.

'Well, we must make sure that he won't get very far, Charlie,' Lane said. 'Now that he's murdered the marshal.' He held aloft the blood-stained knife he had murdered Jackson with. 'Found this stuck in the marshal's gut.

'Anyone see Hadley?'

'Right here, Mr Lane,' came the reply from the shadows, as Jess Hadley stepped forward.

'Where the hell have you been?' Lane questioned the gun-slinger sternly.

'Figured I'd cover your back, boss,'

he said. 'What with everyone rushing about the place, I figured I'd hang around just in case someone decided to take advantage of the chaos to try and kill you. My understanding of this town, in the brief time I've been here, is that those in favour of your plans and those opposed are split about even, and that leaves a sizeable number of folk who, if you don't mind my saying so, Mr Lane, would like to see you dead.'

'Is that a fact,' Lane growled.

The assembled men shifted uneasily. No one had had the gall to talk to Lane in the way the gunfighter had just now, and therefore Lane's reaction was unpredictable.

'Now, given the situation in this town,' Jess Hadley continued, 'I figured that the bruhaha in the marshal's office might have been intended to stir trouble that a sneak assassin could take advantage of, with you left high and dry of protection, Mr Lane.'

Jess Hadley's critical gaze settled on the Lane hardcases.

'Seems to me that you need someone in this outfit that uses his head as well as his gun, boss.'

Samuel Lane's change of mood was dramatic.

'You're right, Jess,' he snarled. 'That's just how it could have been.'

Samuel Lane's gaze joined the gunfighter's to load scorn on the men who were now, knowing Lane's unforgiving nature and quickfire temper, shifting even more uneasily, each man jostling to sink back into the crowd to avoid been singled out.

Lost for words, Lane strode away to the saloon.

'A word, Mr Lane?' Hadley said.

'Sure, Jess.'

Jess Hadley followed Lane to his office.

'I've been thinking, Mr Lane — '

'You think a lot, don't you, Jess,' Lane interjected. 'In fact I never met a gunfighter before who thought as much as you do.'

'Those are the ones who are pushing

up daisies, Mr Lane. Because, you see, a gun doesn't win every argument. Now a man with a fast brain and a fast gun . . . Well, he could live into old age, as I'm counting on doing.'

Samuel Lane went behind his desk and sat down, his eyes never leaving Jess Hadley.

'OK,' he said. 'What's in that thinking mind of yours, Jess?'

'The Moon Raiders,' Hadley stated.

'What about them?' Lane asked, surprised by the subject matter. He had figured that Hadley had witnessed his visit to the marshal's office, had checked on the outcome of that visit, and was contemplating blackmail as a way to quick riches.

'Well, with this meeting you're planning for tomorrow night about the railroad, folk might be upset by a visit from the Moon Raiders to this Blanchard fella's ranch . . . '

'You figure?' Lane asked thoughtfully.

'If the meeting goes against you — '

'It won't,' Lane said confidently, with

a sly smile. 'I've planned well.'

'All the more reason, I say, that you hold off on the Moon Raiders tonight.'

Lane's scrutiny of Jess Hadley was long and hard. Hadley returned Lane's look unflinchingly. 'Never before knew a gunman who spurned a chance to use his gun, Jess,' Lane observed.

'The important thing right now, as I see it, Mr Lane, is that you get approval for your plans for this town. Once that happens,' Jess Hadley grinned, 'then the fun can begin and old scores can be settled.' He drew his sixgun and rolled the chamber, 'the Jess Hadley way.'

11

Jeb Tierney did not break stride until he was well clear of town and certain that he was not being pursued, and that absence of pursuit puzzled him greatly. Perhaps Samuel Lane's wiser counsel had prevailed and Jackson had drawn in his horns. Maybe Lane did not want the kind of trouble that locking him up would stir, just ahead of the meeting at which he was hoping to persuade folk to back his plans for the town and the valley. Tierney did not know the extent of the divide between those who backed Lane's proposal and those who opposed it, but he figured that there was a very thin dividing line between the opposing camps. Hanging Lane's main opponent on a trumped up charge of murder might just swing the scales against him.

★ ★ ★

'Good liquor, Mr Lane,' Jess Hadley complimented his employer, drinking liberally of the Kentucky Rye Samuel Lane had poured.

With Clark dead, Lane could afford to be generous without having the worry of trouble in camp between the gunfighters.

'So Tierney got the drop on Jackson, huh?' Hadley pondered. 'Hardly seems likely, Tierney being a sodbuster.'

'Oh, it was Tierney all right. Frank Jackson told me with his dying breath that it was Tierney who done for him.'

'And Clark, too.' Jess Hadley shook his head in wonder. 'Longer a fella lives, the more surprising life becomes.'

'Another drink, Jess?' Lane invited expansively.

'Well now, don't mind if I do, Mr Lane.'

Lane poured a very generous helping of rye.

'Drink up, Jess,' he said sociably. 'Then you'd best ride out to Tierney's place and hang him for the marshal's murder, Darkie Clark's too. You know what's a real pity,' he growled. 'That we can only hang that bastard Jeb Tierney once.'

He turned to face Hadley, his face grim.

'I want you to lead the posse, Jess. And I guess you'd better wear a star.'

Jess Hadley's grin widened. 'Always wondered what a star would feel like on my shirt, Mr Lane.'

★ ★ ★

Martha Tierney and Lucy Galt came to the cabin door on hearing Jeb's arrival in the yard. Martha immediately sensed trouble.

'What is it, Jeb?' she enquired edgily. 'Something happen in town?'

'Nothing much,' he said, breezing past.

'What's nothing much?' Martha pressed.

'Jackson tried to arrest me for Darkie Clark's murder.'

'Why would he do that?' was Lucy Galt's question.

'That's easy to figure, Lucy,' Jeb said sourly. 'I guess that Jackson reckoned that with me out of the way, a lot of those who believed in my reasoning would fold and come Lane's way. As I went to a cell I rounded on Jackson, laid into him. When he was out cold I hightailed it out the rear of the jail while Lane's rowdies were trying to break down the front door of the law office.

'I almost made it out of town, but one of Lane's hardcases spotted me and I left under a hail of lead.'

'Oh, Jeb,' Martha drew him into her arms. 'Let's stop all this nonsense and just move on, honey. I don't want you killed.'

He distanced her to arm's length.

'Martha Tierney,' he said, in a ringing voice, 'I've never run from any man, and I'm not going to start now.'

'Lucy, will you talk sense to this man of mine,' Martha pleaded.

'There's a lot in what Martha's said,' Lucy counselled. 'This valley and this farm won't be any good if you're lying under it. How did you get in to this mess in the first place, Jeb? Didn't you tell the marshal that you had me as a witness to what happened?'

'I didn't want to get you involved, Lucy. These are dangerous times and dangerous men. It's over fifty miles to honest law in the person of Jake Smallwood over in Abbey Falls. Might as well be on the moon,' he said sourly. 'There's not a trail out of these parts that a Lane no-good ain't watching. We'll get our chance to argue our case tomorrow night at the meeting that Lane called. You know, calling that meeting might just be the mistake I've been waiting for Samuel Lane to make. It'll give us a chance to set the record straight.

'Thing is, I'm not against the railroad as such, though it will grieve me to have track running through the valley. What I'm fearful of is the dregs that the railroad will bring to town.'

'I'm not sure I can back you, Jeb,' Lucy said quietly.

Tierney's stare was hostile. Martha Tierney's reaction was one of total surprise.

'I see,' he said, his tone unfriendly. 'Jess Hadley's really turned your head, ain't he.'

'You and Hadley, Lucy?' Martha said, surprise turning to shock.

'No, Martha. That's Jeb's slant on happenings in town today at the *Gazette* office.'

'I saw with my own eyes how Hadley charmed you, Lucy,' Tierney said accusingly.

'It's got nothing to do with Jess Hadley,' Lucy intoned, frustratedly. 'It's that I happen to think that the arrival of the railroad might not be the disaster that you're making it out to be, Jeb.' She stiffened, every inch now Ned Galt when his stubborn streak came to the fore. 'In fact, I think that the railroad will put Wayne Creek on the map.'

'That it will,' Tierney flung back. 'But for all the wrong reasons!'

'Isn't there some way that we can have the railroad and our town as well?' Martha Tierney said.

'Maybe if we had a crackerjack honest marshal,' Tierney said. 'But I can't see anyone round here who would measure up to the job by a long shot.'

'What stand would you figure that Ned would have taken, Lucy?' Martha asked.

Lucy Galt's answer was instant.

'I figure it would match Jeb's pretty much,' she said. 'Like Jeb, Pa worked hard to make Wayne Creek a family town. A place where women could walk the streets without being ogled or harrassed; a place where children could be reared in safety and with a fear of God's wrath, but also an understanding of His compassion and mercy.'

'My kind of town,' Jeb Tierney said.

'There's got to be someone or some way to solve this problem,' Martha said, her shoulders drooping disconsolately.

'There's just got to be!'

A fast rider thundered into the yard. Jeb Tierney grabbed a rifle and went to the door, opening it a crack.

'State your business and be quick about it,' he called out.

'It's me, Jeb,' a voice called out.

'Luke Blanchard? Is that you?'

'Yeah,' the voice confirmed.

Tierney opened the cabin door. 'What the heck are you doing tearing round the place at this hour of night, Luke?'

'You've got to make tracks and fast, Jeb,' Blanchard said, striding towards the house.

'Make tracks?'

'My boy was in town during all that excitement you stirred up. And when he left, Jess Hadley was rounding up a posse to hunt you down.'

'No need to worry, Luke,' Jeb Tierney reassured his friend and neighbour. 'I've got Lucy as a witness to what happened in Croker's Canyon.'

'I don't know anything about that,

Jeb,' Blanchard said. 'Hadley's posse is coming to get you for the murder of Marshal Jackson.'

Jeb Tierney staggered back.

'I didn't murder Jackson. I laid into him, sure. But he was alive when I left town.'

'Well, if he was, it wasn't for long. Samuel Lane found the marshal dead when he called on him, and the word is that you killed him.'

'This is a set up, Luke,' Tierney stated unequivocally.

'I don't doubt that it is, Jeb,' Blanchard agreed. 'But that won't stop them hanging you. I've got a line shack you can hide out in. Or maybe you should head across the border?'

'I ain't running, Luke,' Tierney declared defiantly. 'I'm no murderer and I ain't going to give anyone cause to think that I am. And that's what will happen if I hightail it now.'

'Luke is right, Jeb,' Martha Tierney pleaded. 'They'll hang you. Probably right here before our very eyes, too.'

Lucy Galt was of the same opinion as Martha and Luke Blanchard.

'Don't you see?' Tierney argued. 'If I don't stand my ground, Lane will present my abscondment as proof positive that I am the killer he claims I am. And that will swing the vote tomorrow night his way.'

'Jeb,' Luke Blanchard said solemnly, 'I admire you as a man and feel privileged that you're my friend, but you're a stubborn cuss who needs a hole drilled in your head and some sense put in!'

The rancher held Tierney's gaze.

'But I'll stand with you, and every Blanchard man, too.'

Jeb Tierney gave a wild yelp of delight.

'That, Luke,' he said, flinging an arm round the rancher's shoulder, 'is the best news I've heard in a long time.'

'The thing is,' Blanchard said, worriedly, 'is that we have to find proof that you did not murder Marshal Jackson to present to a court of law.'

'Court of law,' the farmer groaned.

'Samuel Lane will rig any trial, Luke. You know that. Besides, I won't live long enough to have my day in court.'

'Jeb's right, Mr Blanchard,' Lucy Galt agreed.

'When you said just now that I had your backing, Luke,' Tierney said, a note of keen disappointment in his voice, 'I figured that we were going to town to run Lane right out of the territory.'

Blanchard's worried eyes popped.

'That would add lawlessness to lawlessness, Jeb.'

'Well, how do *you* suggest that we rid the territory of Lane's malign influence, Luke? He ain't going to roll over if we ask him nicely.'

'Have sense, Jeb,' Blanchard said crossly. 'I've got fifteen men, including my boy. Add me and it makes sixteen — '

'Seventeen, with me counted in,' Tierney interjected.

Luke Blanchard's face showed a flush of annoyance.

'Lane's got thirty men or more,' the rancher pointed out.

'Greater disadvantages have been overcome,' Tierney argued.

'Thirty gun-handy men,' Blanchard countered. 'And he's got one of the fastest guns and the meanest coyote in the West in Jess Hadley. You can't seriously expect a bunch of ranch hands to go up against opposition like that, Jeb. It would be plain suicide.

'And what if Andy catches lead? He's the only heir I have to pass on what I've built these last twenty years.'

Jeb Tierney sighed wearily.

'You're right, of course, Luke,' he conceded. 'So that's why I'm going to town alone.'

Martha Tierney blanched.

'No, Jeb. Head across the border until this mess is cleared up.'

'We could send for a US marshal to investigate, Jeb,' Lucy Galt proposed.

Tierney threw cold water on Lucy's suggestion.

'It would take way too long for a US

marshal to arrive. And by then there would be nothing left to investigate. Lane would likely send Hadley after me, and I wouldn't fool myself for a second that his mission would not be successful. And Samuel Lane would have had time to sweep the dirt under the carpet and out of sight. By the time a US marshal would reach town, Lane would make damn sure that there was nothing he could prove. Or no-one he could talk to who would tell him how it was.'

Jeb Tierney's chin set resolutely.

'No. This was always going to be my fight, I guess. Just me against Lane.'

Another round of appeals was about to begin, but were interrupted by the sound of horses coming into the yard at a fast clip.

'That'll be the posse, I reckon,' Jeb said, and walked to the door.

'Wait,' Blanchard said. 'I'll go first to set the terms of your surrender, Jeb. Then I'll ride with you to town. And don't give me any sass,' he bellowed, when Tierney was about to protest. 'Damn heroes!' he grumbled, going outside, 'more trouble than you're worth!'

'Who's leading this poss — ?'

A shot rang out and the rancher fell back in the door.

'Holster that gun!' Jess Hadley ordered the shooter.

On hearing Hadley's reprimand, Jeb Tierney wondered again about an action that was out of character for the notorious killer.

'Mr Lane — '

'Is back in town,' Hadley interjected to silence the man who had shot Blanchard. 'I'm ramrodding this posse, and you'll, all of you, will do as I say. Understood? Understood?' he repeated again, and got a mumble of voices.

'Inside the house,' he called out. 'How is that man?'

Tierney stepped into the open door. 'Flesh wound. He'll live. No thanks to you and the scum you're riding with, Hadley.'

'He stepped out unannounced,' Hadley said. 'That was the act of a fool in my book, Tierney. And, of course, if you hadn't killed Marshal Jackson and Darkie Clark, then none of this would be happening.'

'I didn't murder Jackson or Darkie Clark,' Jeb protested. 'I went to town to tell him that Darkie Clark tried to bushwhack me — '

'And I can verify that, Mr Hadley,' Lucy Galt piped up. 'I was right there with Jeb.'

' . . . Jackson figured that he'd pin Clark's murder on me,' Tierney continued. 'I laid into him. But when I left he was alive, though not kicking. He was murdered after that, and I reckon that it was Lane who did the killing.

'Don't you see? Lane murdered Jackson to see me hang for it.'

Jess Hadley leaned on his saddle horn.

'You want me to believe that you got the drop on Darkie Clark?' he scoffed.

The idea brought a guffaw from

Lane's hardcases.

'No. I didn't nail Clark.'

'Then who did?' one of the men asked.

'A mysterious helper,' Tierney said.

'I've heard mossy yarns afore,' the man sneered. 'But that's the mossiest yet, mister.'

A rider behind Hadley dangled a rope.

'Don't see why we can't settle this right here and now, Jess,' he said. 'He's guilty as hell, and it would save a whole lot of trouble, what with the railroad bosses due to visit town the day after tomorrow.'

Jess Hadley shook his head in wonder.

'That's really dumb, Barrett,' he rebuked the potential rope-slinger. 'Now what impression do you reckon a lynching would give those fine railroad gents, huh?'

He turned back to Jeb Tierney.

'No.' He grinned charmingly. 'We'll have a trial and then hang him. Though as Barrett said, at another time, quick justice would save a whole pile of trouble. Mount up, Tierney. You're under arrest for Frank Jackson's murder.'

'What gives you the right to arrest me for anything?' Tierney challenged Hadley.

'This,' he growled. Jess Hadley flashed the star Lane had pinned on him.

'Figures,' Tierney flung back. 'One snake for another!'

More riders charged into the yard.

'Howdy, Mr Tierney,' Andy Blanchard hailed, most of the Blanchard ranch hands drawing rein behind him. 'We,' his glance included every Blanchard man, 'figured that you might be having company that you wouldn't want around.'

'Looks like there's going to be a lot of lead slung,' was Jess Hadley's observation.

'If that's the way you want it, Hadley,' Andy Blanchard flung back.

Tension crackled in the night air.

'Thanks, Andy,' Jeb Tierney said. 'I surely appreciate your help. But there'll be no shooting.'

'That's real sensible, Tierney,' Hadley said.

'We can take them, Mr Tierney,' Andy Blanchard said. 'Where's Pa,' he asked, glancing around anxiously.

'Inside the house,' Tierney said. 'Took a bullet, but he's OK. Flesh wound.'

'What bastard shot him?' The young rancher's fiery eyes scanned the Lane riders. 'Own up, you coward,' he bellowed when there was no admission. Andy Blanchard drew his rifle from its saddle scabbard and pointed it at the man nearest to him. 'Was it you?'

'Naw,' the man quickly responded.

'Then tell me who it was, or I'll kill you instead!'

'It was him!'

The terrified man pointed to another man to his left. Without hesitation, Andy Blanchard drew a bead on the man.

'No, Andy.' Luke Blanchard came from the house.

'I can drop him right now, Pa,' Andy said.

'Take your pa home, Andy,' Jeb Tierney advised. 'You're too good a man to kill in cold-blood.' He strode to his horse and vaulted into the saddle. 'I'm ready, Hadley.'

'How can you ride for a cur like Samuel Lane?' Lucy hotly questioned Jess Hadley.

'Well, ma'am,' he drawled. 'You see, my gun is for hire. And right now Mr Lane's the highest bidder for my services. Plain and simple as that.'

'Aren't you afraid that you'll rot in hell for your evil misdeeds?'

'Hell might be a long way off or just round the corner, don't know. But I figure that since I came out of the womb of a whore, and had a pa who was hanged as a horsethief, then I was the devil's spawn anyway. So you see, ma'am, when I die old Nick will be welcoming home one of his own.'

He tipped his hat.

' 'Night ma'am.'

Infuriated, Lucy Galt picked up a rock and flung it at Jess Hadley. The missile hit him on the shoulder.

'Darn it,' Lucy fumed. 'That was meant to dent your skull.'

Jeb Tierney quickly swung his horse to place himself between the gunfighter and Lucy, fearing Hadley's retribution for her assault on him. However, the gunfighter's good-humoured response was completely at odds with what one might expect from the kind of mean-minded and vicious killer Hadley was.

'I'd suggest that you practise some before you take a husband, ma'am,' he chuckled. 'No point in wasting good delph when you throw it.'

'I wouldn't have a man under my feet!' Lucy Galt declared spiritedly.

'Sure you will,' Hadley said. 'When the right man comes along.'

He swung his horse and led the posse out of the yard.

'Isn't that the strangest thing,' Lucy said. 'Jess Hadley behaving like a gentleman.'

'Beats me,' Luke Blanchard said, with a shake of his head.

12

Though it was well past the time when most folk in a western town would have retired for the night when Jess Hadley and the posse with Jeb Tierney as its prisoner arrived back in town, the boardwalks had many curious onlookers, who crowded round the door of the marshal's office when the new marshal of Wayne Creek led Tierney into the jail.

'When're we going to hang Tierney, Marshal?' one of Samuel Lane's agents demanded to know, surprised as he was that Tierney had reached town still sucking air.

'After a fair trial,' Hadley replied.

'The saloon is free now,' the agent said, a gent by the name of Charles Bracken, the town lawyer. 'And,' he looked about, 'I count at least a double jury right here.'

'We'll need a judge,' Hadley said.

Bracken went along with what he took to be the gunfighter's pretence of being an honest badge-toter for the benefit of those who were not already aware of Lane's plan to hang Tierney for Jackson's murder. He reckoned that if Jess Hadley ever hung up his gun, he was a damn good enough actor to join a group of touring players.

'It would take at least a month and probably a lot longer for a judge to reach town,' Bracken pointed out. 'So I suggest that I, being a lawyer, and having forgotten more law that most judges ever learned, should act as judge.'

Standing on the saloon porch listening to the exchanges between the town lawyer and Jess Hadley, Samuel Lane was in admiration of their theatrics. If he had not coached Charles Bracken before Hadley's return, and did not know better, he would have had no difficulty in believing his and Hadley's antics to be above board.

'We'll wait for a proper judge,' was Hadley's stern response to Bracken's proposition.

Lane shirked his lazy lounge against a veranda support and came sharply upright, alarmed by Jess Hadley's overplaying. He was changing the mood of the crowd from one of quick justice to one of budding righteousness that could easily flare to resistance and a demand for a proper trial with all the embarrassing questions that would bring, instead of the rigged route to a noose that he had in mind.

Charles Bracken, too, was surprised by Jess Hadley's rejection of his offer to act as a judge, which he had expected him to readily accept. If he did not know better, he would have sworn that the gunfighter's last statement was the unvarnished truth. But he did know better. Hadley was a Lane hireling, overacting his role, dangerously so in his opinion. He was right there in the middle of the crowd, which was getting bigger by the second, and he could sense the shift in their mood. Worried, he glanced back at Lane, whose furious reaction was evident on his tight-lipped face.

He had better get Hadley back on track right away.

'I can understand your desire to have a properly appointed judge, Marshal Hadley,' Charles Bracken said suavely, 'and indeed admire your dedication, sir . . .'

Worryingly, the crowd murmured their agreement.

' . . . However, with such a clear cut case of murder for Tierney to answer, I really am of the opinion that sending for a judge and wasting his time on a case that can have only one verdict, when there is so much lawlessness in the territory to occupy his services, would be a great waste of scarce resources.'

The crowd murmured their agreement again, in response to what they saw as Charles Bracken's down to earth pragmatism. Lane, relieved, leaned back against the veranda support and drew deeply on the cigar he was smoking.

Bracken, too, relaxed, reckoning that he had retrieved a situation which had come perilously close to being lost a few moments before. With Tierney now most assuredly bound for a rope, the thorn in Samuel's Lane's side which had threatened to fester, would be plucked. And shortly, even the crumbs from Lane's table would make him the wealthy man he had always wanted to be. That achieved, he would quit the stinking West and head for the civilized society of Boston where he would marry well and begin the dynasty that one day would provide a President of the United States of America.

However, his plans again threatened to go up in smoke when Jess Hadley stupidly persisted in overplaying his role.

'I'm surely grateful for your kind offer to stand in for a proper judge, Mr Bracken,' he said. 'But,' he held Bracken's gaze, 'as marshal, it's my duty to see that Mr Tierney gets every opportunity to defend himself.

'As a lawyer, I'm sure you'll understand my concerns that justice be seen to be done,' Hadley finished.

'Ah . . . Of course, Marshal,' Bracken mumbled, his surprise too great to overcome.

This time, Samuel Lane remained leaning against the veranda support, because his legs were suddenly too weak to support him.

Jeb Tierney's astonishment was even greater than Samuel Lane's.

'Time to put you in a cell, Tierney,' Jess Hadley said.

A couple of minutes later, the crowd having drifted away, Charles Bracken, fury now replacing surprise, let himself into Lane's office from the alley entrance.

'What the hell is Hadley up to, Samuel?' was his angrily barked question.

'That, Bracken, I intend to ask him right now. Harry,' Lane bellowed. A man popped his head in the door from the saloon. 'Go over to the jail and tell Hadley I want to see him right now.'

'Sure thing, Mr Lane.' Grinning smugly, he asked: 'Hadley's in trouble ain't he?' Darkie Clark had been a good friend of Harry Baum's, and he would wish for nothing better than to see Jess Hadley on the receiving end of Lane's considerable temper.

'You stay put when Hadley leaves,' Lane ordered Baum. 'I don't want to give that bastard Tierney any chance of busting out, or being busted out!'

Harry Baum left and gleefully delivered Samuel Lane's ultimatum to Jess Hadley a moment later, adding:

'I figured all 'long that you were playin' some game of yer own, Hadley. But I reckon that now you've overplayed your hand.'

'Get out, Baum,' Hadley growled. 'You're fouling the air.'

'Darkie Clark was a good friend of mine, Hadley. And I'm goin' to dance me an Irish jig when I see you danglin' from a rope.'

'Won't happen, Baum,' Hadley chuckled. 'Because if that ever happens, you'll be too damn old to wiggle your toes, or long burning in hell.'

'Mr Lane wants to see you right now, Hadley.' Baum's delight at the trouble about to land on Hadley's head danced feverishly in his muddy eyes. 'Said that I was to watch your prisoner while you was with him.'

He sniggered.

'Seems to me that Mr Lane is goin' to chew you out good and proper. Mebbe even send you packin', Hadley.'

Jess Hadley stood up, his six feet towering over Harry Baum's five foot eight, made smaller still by his crouching pose on feeling threatened by the gunfighter.

'No one sends Jess Hadley packing, mister, unless Jess Hadley feels like leaving of his own free will.' He swept past Baum who danced aside, anxious not to impede Hadley's determined departure. He paused before leaving to issue a warning to Lane's lackey: 'I'll expect Tierney to be still unharmed when I get back, Baum. If he's not, I'll take it out of your hide.'

When Hadley arrived at Lane's office, his employer had a scowl that would have scared Satan. Charles Bracken fidgeted with his pocket watch, checking the time every couple of seconds, anxious to be anywhere but where he was. Not a brave man, the lawyer was nervous of being in the company of men who, should the occasion call for it, kill without qualm. And he also worried that his link to Lane, though long suspected, was now firmly established. Normally his meetings with Lane were held at dead of night or outside of town in secret places, and he now bitterly regretted having allowed his anxiety to overrule his judgement by coming directly to Lane after the fiasco outside the marshal's office. But, though there was as yet no strong evidence, he had a sense of matters going radically wrong, and was imaginative enough to see an end result to his association with Samuel Lane that would not in the least be to his liking.

'That weasel Baum said you wanted to see me, Mr Lane?'

Jess Hadley's question was in no way subservient. In fact, Lane noted that Hadley's mood was close to dismissive. His take it or leave it attitude infuriated Lane.

'What the hell game do you think you're playing at, Hadley?' he barked.

Jess Hadley shrugged.

'Game, Mr Lane?'

'Why isn't that bastard Tierney's neck in a noose?'

Charles Bracken flinched. Such blunt speech by Samuel Lane in his presence, drew him into a circle in which he did not want to be. He had gone out of his way to avoid, in the presence of witnesses, any discussion about what needed to be done for Lane to get a stranglehold on the town and valley, and the benefits that would flow to him as a result. Because if Lane's scheme backfired, and the law, in the form of a US marshal was assigned to investigate Lane's antics, there would be a lot of people scurrying around pointing the finger to divert attention from their own involvement. And the town lawyer would be a coveted prize for any such investigator to nab.

'I didn't even expect to see him back in town,' Lane added. 'I figured that the problem of Jeb Tierney would have been solved along the way, Hadley.'

'Well, the way I see it, Mr Lane,' Hadley drawled, 'Tierney's hanging has got to seem above board to avoid the risk of anyone lodging a protest against a lynching. That could bring all sorts of problems down the line.'

'I agree,' Charles Bracken said eagerly.

'No one asked if you agree or disagree, Bracken!' Lane barked.

Bracken wiped away the sudden sweat which Lane's angry rebuke brought to his brow.

'And you've got that vote to win

tomorrow night,' Hadley reminded Lane.

'Don't you worry about the vote. It's already won.'

'It is?' Hadley asked.

'Did you notice men drifting into town today?' Lane asked Hadley.

'I've been curious,' he replied.

'When that vote is taken tomorrow night, all those fellas I've brought into town will swing the vote my way.' He chuckled. 'Nothing like a little insurance to give a man peaceful nights. So, you see, hanging Tierney this minute won't make a difference, Jess.'

'I guess not, in the short term,' Hadley agreed. 'But once this town is won, then comes the job of keeping it.'

'That's why I've hired fellas like you.'

Jess Hadley shook his head sagely.

'No amount of hired guns can keep a town, if the citizens of that town rise up.'

'Lead is a great persuader,' Lane said, and opined: 'I'm not planning on any revolt.'

'I've seen towns like this before, Mr Lane,' Jess Hadley said. 'Hired out in quite a few of them. And it was always the same. Folk pushed too far will fight back. And when they do, there's always a whole pile of bodies.

'Always including the body of the man who figured that there would be no revolt,' he grimly pointed out.

Samuel Lane swallowed hard.

'Now, if you want my advice . . . ?'

'I'm sure the advice of a man of Mr Hadley's profession and undoubted stature in that profession would be very valuable, Samuel,' Charles Bracken said with breathless nervousness.

'Talks like he's swallowed a damn dictionary, don't he,' Lane sneered. He settled a probing gaze on Jess Hadley. 'What might this advice be?'

'Let Tierney walk — '

'Walk!' Lane exploded. 'What kind of crazy advice is that?'

'As I understand it, Tierney's got a lot of friends . . . ?'

'That's true,' Bracken confirmed.

'Friends who'll never be persuaded that he's a cold-blooded killer . . . '

'Mr Hadley's right, Samuel,' the lawyer counselled.

'And when Lucy Galt arrives back in town in the morning to back Tierney's story about how Darkie Clark tried to bushwhack them — '

'Good grief!' Charles Bracken swayed and clutched at the side of Lane's desk to steady himself as his head spun.

'Lucy Galt?' Samuel Lane said, concerned.

'She was right there in Croker's Canyon when Clark tried to kill Tierney,' Hadley stated.

'Then we'll have to kill her as well,' was Samuel Lane's panicked solution. Charles Bracken lost his battle to remain standing, and fell to the floor with a whimper. 'Leave him be,' Lane growled, when Hadley went to the lawyer's assistance.

'Dispatching Tierney carries its risks, Mr Lane,' he said. 'But killing Lucy Galt would have this town screaming for blood — yours, I reckon.'

'I've got enough firepower to — '

'Don't fool yourself,' Hadley interjected. 'First sign of trouble and most of the men on your payroll would have their butts in leather and riding hard before you could blink.'

'And you?' Lane questioned Hadley.

'I'm one gun, Mr Lane,' Hadley sighed. 'No matter how fast I can shoot, I'll never be able to shoot fast enough to stop a howling mob.'

Lane sprang out of his chair and began pacing the office. 'When Lucy Galt backs Tierney's story about Darkie Clark trying to murder him — '

'And her,' Hadley pointed out.

' — Who do you think everyone will come looking for?'

'You can always say Clark acted on his own. Tierney's had plenty of run-ins with him, ain't he?'

'I've lost count.' Seeing a glimmer of light at the end of the tunnel, Lane said: 'Yeah. You're right, Jess. Shouldn't be too difficult to spin a yarn to make folk believe that Clark acted on his own.'

'I reckon not, Mr Lane.'

'What about Jackson's murder?'

'Someone will surely have to hang for that,' Hadley said. 'You figuring on being a candidate?'

'Me?'

'Well, you killed him.' Lane's eyes narrowed to slits. 'When we went to the marshal's office and found him dead, his blood was still warm and fresh, not congealed the way it would have been had Jeb Tierney murdered him.'

'You're a real clever fella, Jess,' Lane said with quiet menace.

Jess Hadley stretched, like a sleepy cat.

'Baum will do,' he said.

'Baum?'

'He doesn't count for anything to anyone,' Hadley said matter-of-factly. 'And if you've got the knife you stuck Jackson with, it shouldn't be difficult to find it in Baum's saddlebag. Now should it?'

All of Samuel Lane's worries vanished.

'Not difficult at all, Jess,' he chuckled.

Jess Hadley stood up. 'Well, you go and arrange that, and we'll have ourselves a neck for that rope you've been so anxious to have slung. That will leave no questions to answer, and you'll be left holding the neatest package you've ever seen, Mr Lane.

'Now, I'll head back to the jail. You drop by in a little while with this story about finding a bloodied knife in Harry Baum's saddlebag. I'll spring Tierney and sling Baum in jail in his place. Then directly after you've got that,' he grinned, '*free* vote to turn this burg into the open town you want it to be, we'll hang Baum for Jackson's murder.'

Hadley was about to leave to return to the jail when Lane said: 'Friend of yours arriving on the stage tomorrow, Jess.'

'Friend of mine, you say?' Hadley enquired warily.

'A real pretty friend, too.' Lane winked lecherously, and drew a curvy shape with his hands. 'Wouldn't mind having her passed on when you're finished, Jess.'

'Does this,' Hadley mimicked Lane's drawing of a curvy shape, 'have a name?'

'Belle Lafontaine.'

Jess Hadley flashed expressive eyes, and exclaimed: 'Belle Lafontaine!'

'She's coming to sing in the saloon. I figure that the kind of custom I'll have pretty soon, will want to be entertained by someone classy.'

'Well, there's none classier than Belle,' Hadley said.

'Belle says you and her were *real cozy* for a couple of months in a burg down near the border called . . . ' Lane scratched his head. 'Damn. What was that name?' He looked to Hadley for enlightment.

'I've been in a lot of burgs down near the border, boss,' Hadley responded.

'How could you forget the name of

the town where you were shacked up with Belle Lafontaine, Jess?' He chuckled. 'I'd remember every speck of darn dust.'

'Look, why don't I give you first option on Belle,' Hadley said.

Samuel Lane was stunned.

'You mean that?' he questioned, obviously expecting a price tag on the gunfighter's offer.

'Sure,' Jess Hadley said, magnanimously. 'Now, there's this little trick she likes to get her really warmed up . . .' He leaned close to Lane to whisper in his ear. Lane's eyes popped. Hadley chuckled. 'Don't tell her I told you. Pretend that you're just that good yourself, and Belle will leave you breathless for days to come.'

Jess Hadley slipped out the door into the alley, still chuckling. However, once outside his laughter ceased abruptly and was replaced by a growling annoyance.

'Who the hell is Belle Lafontaine!'

13

Jeb Tierney was woken by the clang of keys in the cell lock. He woke to find Jess Hadley bearing down on him. 'Stand up, Tierney.' Shaken, Jeb did as he was told. It was past midnight. The streets would be deserted, except for the odd straggler making his way home from the saloon, the perfect time for mischief. The possible use for the sixgun which Jess Hadley was holding was not lost on Tierney. A bullet in the back as the prisoner tried to escape was a well tested method of getting rid of a troublesome prisoner. 'You're free to go, Tierney,' he stated, and when the farmer stayed put, Hadley enquired crossly: 'What are you waiting for? I said you're — '

'I heard you, Hadley,' Jeb Tierney replied curtly. 'But I figure I'm safer right here with my back to the wall.'

Jess Hadley glanced at the Colt he was holding.

'You think I'm going to shoot you in the back while you're breaking out, right?'

'The thought did cross my mind, *Marshal*.'

'This,' Jess Hadley held up the sixgun, 'is for the prisoner who'll be replacing you as noose-fodder,' he explained.

'Replacing me?'

'Marshal Jackson's real killer.'

On cue, Samuel Lane appeared holding up an almost unconscious Harry Baum, blood streaming from a wound on the side of his head from Lane's gunbutt.

'Had to sedate the prisoner, Marshal,' Lane sneered.

'Baum didn't murder Jackson,' Tierney proclaimed, and looked unflinchingly at Lane. 'He did!'

'Now where's your proof of that?' Hadley challenged.

'I figure that during the commotion

my departure from town stirred up, Lane grabbed the opportunity to murder Jackson to put the blame on me, as a way of getting that thorn I've become out of his side.'

Samuel Lane ran a finger inside the collar of his shirt, as if it had suddenly become too small, confirming for Jeb Tierney his suspicions.

'You know, Tierney,' Hadley said, slapping his thigh, 'you're a real imaginative sort of fella. Now,' his tone became granite hard, 'get your butt out of that cell and back to your farm! Don't see any reason for you to worry about whose neck will replace yours in a noose.'

'I guess you're right at that, Hadley,' he agreed. 'Why the hell should I worry.'

'Sensible,' Hadley commented.

Though Jeb Tierney put on a show of indifference, he was far from feeling indifferent to Baum's plight. Harry Baum might not be much of a man, but that did not give anyone the right to hang him for a murder he did not commit. He tucked in his shirt and donned his hat, brushing back the thick black hair.

'If you say that Baum murdered Jackson, that's good enough for me, Marshal. I've surely got enough on my plate trying to keep my farm from going under.'

'There's no need for all that blood, sweat and tears, Tierney,' Lane said. 'My offer for your land is still on the table.'

'You know,' the farmer said, heavy shouldered, 'I might just take you up on that offer, Lane.'

'My door is open, Tierney.'

Jess Hadley grabbed Baum, who was regaining his wits and beginning to struggle with Lane, and shoved him into the cell which Tierney had just vacated and slammed the cell door.

'I didn't kill no one, Mr Lane,' Baum whined. 'And I don't know nothin' 'bout that knife in my saddlebag.'

'Shut up, Baum,' Hadley growled.

'You're Frank Jackson's killer and there's no doubt about it.' He sneered. 'And you're going to hang for it.'

'Please, Mr Tierney,' Baum pleaded. 'You've got to get me outta here.'

Jeb Tierney shrugged.

'Better your neck in a noose than mine, Baum,' he said, and left.

'That went well, I reckon,' Hadley said to Lane, looking after Tierney as he rode out of town. 'Looks like Tierney is ready to accept your offer, and we've got a man to string up for Jackson's murder. A good night's work, I'd say.'

'Together, we can run this entire damn territory, Jess,' Lane said, pleased as punch. 'I'm sure glad that my letter caught up with you, and that you decided to hire out to me.'

Jess Hadley arched his back and stretched.

'Reckon I'll get some shuteye now, boss,' he said. 'It's been a busy night.'

Lane yawned. 'I'm kind of beat myself.' He strolled away. 'Be seeing you, Jess. Be sure not to miss the noon stage to greet Belle Lafontaine.'

After Samuel Lane had left, Jess Hadley dropped into his chair, and became deeply thoughtful. Then he stood up and looked at his image in the shaving mirror on the wall behind the desk. After a long study, he murmured:

'Maybe, if I keep my left hand in my pocket, Belle Lafontaine will be fooled.'

14

Martha Tierney and Lucy Galt were astounded when Jeb Tierney put in an appearance. Both women assumed that he had broken out of jail, until he told them otherwise.

'Hadley just let you go?' Lucy asked, astonished.

'Why?' Martha enquired.

'It's my guess that Jess Hadley was behind the idea to exchange Harry Baum for me as ropefodder.'

'Baum?' Lucy said. 'Baum wouldn't have the wits to commit murder. He's only got nuisance value. Anyone can see that, Jeb.'

'I figure that it was Samuel Lane who murdered Jackson to have me hanged for it. Kill two birds with the one stone. Get rid of Jackson, and hand his badge to Jess Hadley. And with me hanged, he'd figure that the opposition to his plans would whither away.'

'You've done enough, Jeb,' Martha said. 'Take Lane's offer and we'll just up and leave this accursed valley behind us.'

'But I can't let an innocent man hang, Martha,' he protested. 'To do that would make me no better than Lane and Hadley.'

Martha clutched at him.

'Jeb, I didn't want to say anything, you having so much on your plate — '

'Say what?' he asked curiously.

'I'm with child, Jeb,' she said, soft tears of joy welling up in her eyes.

After an astonished moment, he grabbed Martha and danced her round the room.

'Steady,' Lucy Galt cautioned, bringing Jeb's crazy dance of joy to a halt. 'You don't want to lose the baby, do you.'

'You're OK, aren't you, honey?' he urgently quizzed Martha.

'I'm fine, Jeb,' she said. 'Just downright dandy!'

'I'll ride into town first thing and take Lane's offer for the farm. We'll be out of here in a week or less, Martha.'

'Of course we will,' Martha said, a touch sad. 'But you're right, Jeb. It wouldn't be proper or good to let Harry Baum hang for a murder he didn't commit.' She took her husband's hands in hers. 'Once that's out of the way, we'll pack up and go.'

He kissed Martha on the cheek.

'You're one fine woman, Martha Tierney,' he said. 'And I'm the luckiest man alive to have you as my wife.'

'Now don't you get all soppy on me, Jeb Tierney,' Martha scolded, but the light shining in her eyes told of how pleased she was. 'I won't know where I stand if you're not grumpy!'

'Go now!' Lucy Galt urged them. 'Samuel Lane will only stand for so much bucking, Jeb. And the fact that he sent Darkie Clark to ambush you and murdered Jackson to hang you, is proof positive that he's reached his limit of tolerance with you.'

'I reckon I can handle Lane,' Jeb said.

'Can you also handle Jess Hadley?' Lucy asked. The slump in Jeb Tierney's shoulders was answer enough. 'He's a killer through and through, Jeb,' she said with a quiet regret.

Martha and Jeb exchanged glances at Lucy Galt's sudden gloom.

'You know,' Lucy said after a spell of deep thought, 'I just don't understand him, Jess Hadley, I mean. There's something about him that is at odds with his reputation, don't you think?'

Her hopeful gaze switched between Martha and Jeb Tierney.

'There is something,' Jeb conceded. 'But what the hell it is, I'm at a loss to know, Lucy.'

'You haven't fallen in love with him, have you, Lucy?' Martha wanted to know.

'In love?' Lucy yelped. 'I hardly know him, Martha. Only spoke to him when he came into the *Gazette* office with Lane's advertisement about the railroad meeting, and that was for no time at all.'

'Takes no time at all to fall in love, Lucy,' Martha said sagely.

Lucy looked away to hide her blushes as she recalled how giddy she had felt when Jess Hadley had come close to her.

'He's a gunfighter,' she murmured. 'A killer. How could I possibly fall in love with a man like that?' She was asking the question of herself as much as putting it to Jeb and Martha.

'A man like that will be no good for you, Lucy,' Martha said. 'He'll bring you grief every day up to the day he dies. Which could be any day, depending on when his luck runs out and someone faster comes along.'

'No!' Lucy declared. 'I am not in love with Jess Hadley!'

Funny how false her spirited outburst sounded to her ears. And looking at Martha and Jeb, she could see that she had not convinced them either.

'Come morning, I'll head over to

Abbey Falls and ask the marshal there to help stop Harry Baum's unjust hanging,' Jeb said.

'And I'll use the *Gazette* to question his detention,' Lucy said.

'And that leaves the praying to me,' Martha Tierney said, worry etched in every line of her face.

15

'An innocent man's life is at stake,' Jeb Tierney pleaded with Jake Smallwood, the marshal of Abbey Falls. 'This is no time to be considering the finer points of jurisdiction. All of that can be ironed out later.'

Smallwood scratched his iron grey head.

'I'd be pretty ticked off, Mr Tierney, if the marshal over in Wayne Creek poked his nose in the affairs of my town. And I'm sure that he'll feel no different.

'I knew Frank Jackson to be an honest lawman,' he stated. He held up his hand to stay Tierney's protest. 'And I know too that he might have gone off the tracks, tempted by this fella Lane. But if the new marshal of Wayne Creek says that he's caught Jackson's killer . . .'

He shrugged.

'The new marshal of Wayne Creek is not your every day variety of lawman,' Jeb said. 'Heard of Jess Hadley, ain't you?'

'Hadley?' What's he got to do with all of this?'

'That gent is now the badge-toter in Wayne Creek.'

'Jess Hadley, a lawman?'

'I said he toted a badge,' Tierney said. 'I said nothing about upholding the law.'

Smallwood sprang out of his chair, went to the door and yanked it open. 'Mike. Get in here,' he ordered.

The man whittling on the porch arrived promptly.

'What is it, Jake?' the deputy enquired of the marshal, his narrowed eyes suspiciously sweeping Jeb Tierney.

'I'm headed over to Wayne Creek. You be sure to put legs under that gambler I've ordered out of town, you hear?'

'I've already told him to be on his way, Jake,' the deputy said, puffing out his chest.

'He's a slippery one,' the marshal warned his deputy. 'Don't blink until his dust is settled.' He grabbed his hat from a crook near the door. 'Let's ride,' he told Tierney.

'What's goin' on over in Wayne Creek, that Frank Jackson can't handle?' the deputy questioned.

'Jackson's dead, and the marshal over in Wayne Creek is Jess Hadley, Mike.'

'Jess Ha-ha-hadley?' the deputy stammered, swallowing hard. 'Hadley ain't no lawman.'

'That's why I'm on my way over there,' Smallwood said, swinging up on his horse and setting a fast pace out of town.

★　★　★

'Stage coming!' The stage depot clerk's voice rang out over the town. And it's only two days overdue,' he boasted.

Samuel Lane, as excited as a kid with candy, burst into the marshal's office. 'Well, come on, Jess. Introduce me nicely to Belle Lafontaine.'

'Sure, Mr Lane,' Hadley said, rising out of his chair to follow Lane.

'I hear tell that Belle Lafontaine is a woman that would stir passion in a dead man,' an old-timer outside the stage depot informed the eagerly waiting crowd, almost entirely male except for a couple of placard bearing women who saw it as their duty to keep sinful influences out of Wayne Creek.

'We don't need her kind of woman in this town,' a matronly figure declared sternly.

'We do when you're all we've got now,' the oldtimer giggled.

'You should be preparing to meet your Maker, Larry Scott,' the woman rebuked him.

'Well, I guess after a glimpse of Belle Lafontaine, I'll be ready to meet Him with a smile, ma'am,' he crowed.

'Seems like Belle is going to be a big hit, Jess,' Lane told Hadley, craning his neck to catch a glimpse of Belle Lafontaine as the stage thundered to a halt in front of the depot, wheels locked, choking dust obliterating his view.

The depot clerk, as anxious as every other man to get a glimpse of Belle Lafontaine, hurried to open the stage door, a duty he would normally leave to a lesser employee.

'Hold on there!' Lane commanded, grabbing the clerk. 'I think it only right that Belle should be greeted first by an old friend,' Hadley cringed, 'our new marshal Jess Hadley. Well, don't hang back, Jess. Don't you want to be first in line?'

'Sure,' Hadley enthused, striding forward to yank open the door of the stagecoach. 'Howdy, Belle,' he greeted, and waited for one of the three women on board to respond, so that he would know who Belle Lafontaine was.

A honey-blond woman with blue eyes as clear as a mountain spring, and a shape that finally made sense of Adam's temptation, stood up. Jess Hadley's mouth was open when a second woman, with straggly red hair, puffy cheeks, muddy eyes and a matronly figure hailed:

'Jess Hadley, you old hound dog!'

Belle Lafontaine rushed forward, knocking the other woman aside, and leapt into Hadley's arms to plant a whiskey-laden kiss on him. Startled glances switched from the blond woman to Belle Lafontaine, and after a brief but disgusted perusal, returned with a sigh to the elegant blond woman as she stepped from the coach and entered the stage depot, fussed over by the stage depot clerk. The woman out of sight, the assembled men returned their disbelieving looks to the wreck of a woman who was Belle Lafontaine with a great deal of pity and no lust at all. But the most surprised and disappointed man of all was Samuel Lane. In seconds, anger predominated, as he thought of the time and money he had spent on the seduction of Belle Lafontaine.

'Put those arms round me, Jess,' Belle said, her whiskied eyes studying him closely. She encircled her waist with Hadley's arms and cuddled up to him 'Who the hell are you and what's your game, fella?' she murmured. 'You're the spit of Jess, sure enough. But you ain't Jess.' After a moment she stepped back and cast her whiskey shod eyes downwards. 'Don't look like you're all that pleased to see me, Jess?' she mocked.

Her mood was jocular, but her eyes showed an ocean of sadness.

'You're Belle Lafontaine?' Lane wailed in disgust. 'Get back on the stage and keep right on going!'

'Get back on the stage?' Belle Lafontaine protested.

'Yes,' Lane bellowed. 'You'd empty my saloon in seconds flat!'

'Are you going to let that mound of horse manure talk to me like that, Jess?' Belle demanded of Hadley.

Moved by pity for the woman who had once packed out saloons, his added rejection to Samuel Lane's cruelty pained him greatly. However, the sooner Belle Lafontaine was out of town the safer he would be.

'I figure Mr Lane's right,' he barked. 'Best keep going, Belle. You're all washed up.'

'Never figured on hearing those words from you, Jess,' Belle Lafontaine said, her gaze digging deep into his soul.

'Go on,' Hadley snarled. 'Get back on board that damn stage and out of my sight, woman!'

'Maybe we should talk first, Jess,' she said.

'What's to talk about?' he flung back.

'Old times, of course,' Belle said, a world of meaning in her voice for his ears.

'Well, I guess talking won't hurt. But when the stage leaves in an hour, you'll be on it for sure, Belle.'

'How can you bear to be anywhere near this whiskey-swilling old hag, Jess?' Lane wondered.

'I'll hold my nose, Mr Lane,' Hadley chuckled.

With heads shaking, men drifted

away, all except the old-timer who had been waiting anxiously to feast his eyes on Belle Lafontaine.

'You know, Marshal. If I was a younger man I'd whup you good and proper for the hurt you caused this poor woman,' he said. 'And if I could use a gun, I'd call you out, damn you to hell!'

Jess Hadley quickly escorted Belle Lafontaine into the marshal's office, and immediately launched in to an explanation.

'My real name is US marshal Jack Crow, ma'am . . . '

'Crow?' Belle exclaimed. 'The one man Jess feared catching up with him.' She shook her head in amazement. 'You could pass for Jess's twin brother.'

'Well, that's what gave me the idea, you see, Belle — '

'What idea was that?'

'When I shot Jess — '

'Jess is dead?' she asked, tears flooding her eyes.

'Yes, Belle. He's dead.'

'So you were faster after all?'

'No, I wasn't. Luck favoured me on the day, Belle.'

'Well, I guess Jess went to hell happy knowing that it was just a twist of fate that dispatched him. Now what was this idea you had after killing Jess, Mr Crow?'

'I found a letter in Jess Hadley's pocket from Samuel Lane, wanting to hire his gun. So I figured that Lane was up to no good, if he wanted Jess on his payroll, and seeing how I looked like Jess, I decided to mosey along to Wayne Creek and find out what devilment Lane was hatching, Belle.'

'And did you find out?'

'Enough to finish Lane,' Crow said. 'But if you don't keep our secret, Belle . . . '

'Have no fear, Mr Crow,' Belle Lafontaine said. 'My reward will be to know that Lane is good and truly cowed.'

'That he will be, I promise you, Belle,' Jack Crow promised.

'Well, I'd best be making tracks for the stage depot again, Mr Crow.'

'How were you so certain right off that I was not Jess?' Crow enquired.

'The small finger of your left hand is all there, Jack. Jess had half of his cut off in a poker game that went sour, just before he rode away from me for the last time.'

'I figured that if I kept my hand in my pocket I could buy enough time to sling Lane in jail.'

'Knowing that you will, will make my nights more restful, Jess. I mean, Jack,' she corrected. She shook her head in wonder. 'You're the very spit of Jess, Marshal Crow, except for the way your fringe curls over your left eye.'

Outside the marshal's office, Lane eased away from the door which Belle Lafontaine had carelessly left an inch open on entering. His look was murderous.

Hadley took some dollar bills from his pocket and pressed them into Belle Lafontaine's hand. She immediately handed them back.

'It's not charity I need, Jack,' she said sadly. Jack Crow drew her to him and kissed her full on the mouth. Belle Lafontaine smiled broadly, if somewhat reflectively. 'Darn it, Jack Crow,' she said. 'You even kiss like Jess Hadley did.'

'You know, Belle, Jess Hadley was a mighty lucky cuss to have known a woman like you,' Crow complimented sincerely.

Belle Lafontaine sighed.

'I kept telling Jess that, but he never would believe it.'

'Then, Belle,' Crow said. 'Jess Hadley had a fast gun, but a darn slow brain.'

⋆　⋆　⋆

In a rage fit to burst a blood vessel, Samuel Lane yanked open the door of his office and bawled into the saloon: 'Lawton. Get in here!' A tall, ungainly man shuffled across the saloon from a game of blackjack. Lane dragged him into the office and slammed the door shut. 'We've got some bloodletting to do, Sam,' he said.

Lawton's eyes lit up. 'Me and the boys was wonderin' when we'd be gettin' down to business, Mr Lane.'

'Right now,' Lane growled, grimly.

16

'Don't move a darn muscle!' Jake Smallwood, the Abbey Falls marshal, held Jack Crow under threat of his sixgun. 'To be truthful, I'm kind of nervy, Hadley.'

'I'm not Jess Hadley,' Crow said.

Smallwood was dismissive.

'You're Hadley all right, mister,' the lawman growled. 'Seen your dial on enough wanted posters.'

'I'm the spit of Hadley, sure enough,' Crow said, 'and the comparison doesn't rest easy with me. But I'm really Jack Crow.'

'The US marshal?' Smallwood scoffed. 'And I'm the King of England.'

'Let him have his say, Marshal Smallwood,' Jeb Tierney urged, recalling the Wayne Creek marshal's inconsistent behaviour with a man of Jess Hadley's character. And when Smallwood was doubtful, added: 'I figure we have nothing to lose by listening.'

'I guess not,' the Abbey Falls lawman agreed. 'But you blink and you're dead,' he warned Crow.

Tierney studied the man who claimed he was US marshal Jack Crow. 'You wouldn't be the feller who shot Darkie Clark, would you?'

'Didn't leave me a choice,' Crow replied. 'Darkie Clark was as rotten an apple as you'll find in any barrel.' Crow took from his vest pocket a crumpled letter and handed it to Smallwood. 'When I killed Jess Hadley, by a pure stroke of luck, I found this letter from Samuel Lane in his pocket.'

As Jake Smallwood read the letter, Crow continued:

'Figured that a man who wanted to hire Hadley had real evil intentions. So, figuring that I could pass myself off as Jess Hadley until I found out what Lane was up to, I moseyed along to Wayne Creek to do just that, and I'm sure glad I did.

'Lane wants to make Wayne Creek an open town. He pinned a badge on me to make sure that the law would back his every dirty trick. But most of all Lane is a cold-blooded killer.'

He looked to Tierney.

'You were right, it was Lane who murdered the marshal. Heaven knows that Jackson brought trouble on his own head by hitching his wagon to Lane's. But that still doesn't excuse Lane's vile act of murder.

'I regret having had to sling you in jail, Tierney. But I reckoned that in jail, you'd be a whole lot safer than roaming free.'

Closer to the window, Jeb Tierney's attention was got by the commotion on the street. He craned his neck to look in the direction everyone on the street was looking and saw Samuel Lane leading a dozen men out of the saloon and across the street, no guessing their destination.

'Trouble,' he said. 'Big trouble.'

Jack Crow and Jake Smallwood joined Tierney at the window, and deciding that the trouble was too big to handle in a direct confrontation, Crow hurried himself and his guests out the back door, collecting a pair of shotguns and a rifle on the way — the rifle he slung to Jeb Tierney.

'Follow me,' Crow said grimly.

Lane's brood of killers burst into the law office, guns drawn and ready for murder. Jack Crow, backed up by Tierney and Smallwood appeared in the street behind them, Greeners primed and Winchester ready.

'Obliging of you fellas to drop by,' Crow said. Startled, Lane and the men with him swung round, immediately recognizing their plight and their stupidity. 'Now, fellas,' Jack Crow said calmly, 'you've got a choice. You can either ride out of town right now. Or you can risk being cut in half by these blunderbuses.

'But you're going nowhere, Lane, except to a gallows for Frank Jackson's murder.'

It took no time at all for the men

directly in line of fire to make up their minds.

'Come back here!' Lane yelled, as they piled out the door. 'I pay your wages.'

'Ain't 'nuff money to pay a man to risk a shotgun, Lane,' the first man to break ranks said.

'Looks like you're all washed up, Lane,' Jack Crow said sternly.

'There's still enough of us to kill you when the load's gone from those blasters, Crow,' Lane said.

'Are you fellas willing to risk being cut in half for Lane?' Crow quizzed the six men who, as yet, had not fled. Crow continued graphically: 'One of these beauties will send bits of you all the way to Mexico.'

'Don't listen to him,' Lane urged breathlessly, as the men looked wide-eyed into the barrels of the shotguns.

'I'm hittin' the trail,' one of the remaining men said, and hurried from the marshal's office.

'Draw that gun and I'll unload hell

on you, Lane,' Crow warned, as Lane's right hand sneaked towards his pistol, his intention to back-shoot the departing man obvious. 'All you other men have got safe passage too,' he added.

In seconds the last of Lane's hardcases were galloping out of Wayne Creek, as if the devil was chasing their souls.

Deserted and panicked, Lane pleaded: 'I'm sure I can do a deal with you gents.'

'The only deal you're in line for, Lane,' Jack Crow said resolutely, 'is a hangman's rope!'

Crow backed Lane to a cell alongside Harry Baum's under threat of the shotgun.

'How does it feel, *Mr* Lane?' Baum mocked the profusely perspiring Lane. 'Kinda leaves you short of breath, don't it. But then you don't have much breath left to breathe an'way.'

'Unbuckle your gunbelt and toss it out,' Crow ordered Lane.

As he was unbuckling his gunbelt,

Baum reached through the cell bars and grabbed Lane's sixgun. Before Jack Crow could blink, he had fired five of its six rounds into Samuel Lane.

'Bastard!' he screamed, and threw the gun at Lane.

'That was a damn silly thing to do,' Jack Crow berated Baum. 'Now you'll have to stay put to hang for Lane's murder.'

'It'll be worth it,' Baum snorted.

The explosion shattered Harry Baum's chest. Crow swung round. It was probably Samuel Lane's last breath, but he had used it to kill Baum with the single bullet of six left in the sixgun that Baum had thrown back at him. Jack Crow reacted instinctively and shattered Lane's head with a bullet right between the eyes.

*   *   *

'What if you folk got your railroad and kept your town as it is?'

The meeting which Lane had arranged

for had gone ahead in an effort to sort out the wrangling for and against the railroad. The gathering went quiet, eager to hear Jack Crow's plan.

'What have you got in mind, Marshal Crow?' Lucy Galt was first to ask.

'A law enforcing committee,' he said. 'Not just a marshal. But a marshal and say four gun-handy men, acting together, to see off any unwanted visitors. Put the hombre right back on the train the instant he steps off.

'Word would soon get out that Wayne Creek was not a town to visit, if other than commerce or honest endeavour was your intention.'

The meeting looked at Jeb Tierney for his reaction, and it pleased him that they should seek his approval or disapproval.

'It's a good plan, Jack,' Jeb Tierney said without hesitation. Instantly the crowd went along with Tierney's endorsement. 'Only for one thing . . . ' he cautioned. Uncertainty again gripped the gathering. 'Where will this town find a marshal of the calibre needed to make this plan work?'

'That's a damn good question,' Luke Blanchard said.

Jeb Tierney held up his hands to silence the din that had broken out. 'Now if Lucy and Jack were to tie the knot, that would mean that Jack would be staying put.'

'What?' Lucy Galt gasped.

'Are you saying that you're not in love with Jack Crow, Lucy?' Tierney challenged.

'I . . . I . . . I . . . ' Lucy blustered.

'I reckon that answers the question, Lucy,' Blanchard called out.

'Jack,' Tierney said, 'might you be in love with Lucy?'

Jack Crow's admission was honest.

'Since the second I walked into the *Gazette* office.'

'Marshal Crow!' Lucy yelped.

'It's true, Lucy,' Crow said. 'And,' he grinned in his heart-stopping way, 'I figure you sparked a little, too.'

Colour as hot as hell's coals spread

relentlessly up Lucy Galt's face. 'You're a very brazen man, Jack Crow,' she said, her blustering ten times worse.

'You know,' Jeb Tierney said, 'I reckon that the only question to be answered now is, when will this town have a wedding party that will raise the roof, folks?'

'I always thought I'd be partial to being a June bride,' Lucy said quietly.

'This is the last day of May!' Jack Crow yelped.

'Getting cold feet, Jack?' Lucy asked, mischief dancing in her green eyes.

'Heck, no,' Crow said. 'June it is, Lucy Galt. That is if you ain't got cold feet?'

'June it is, Jack Crow,' she replied smugly.

Crow returned his attention to the meeting. 'Now, there's only one obstacle remaining to us getting that rail spur, and that's the land over which the track will run.'

All eyes switched to Jeb Tierney for his response.

'No problem there, Jack,' Tierney said. 'There'll still be plenty of land either side of the track to farm and ranch. The only thing is ... ' He hugged Martha to him. 'Anyone know if passing trains will wake a baby?'

A rousing cheer lifted the rafters.

'Well, at least you won't have any Moon Raiders to worry about, Jeb,' Jack Crow said, taking Lucy in his arms to kiss her.

The rafters of the Bucking Buffalo saloon proved their stoutness as cheer was added to cheer.

THE END

We do hope that you have enjoyed reading this large print book.

Did you know that all of our titles are available for purchase?

We publish a wide range of high quality large print books including:
Romances, Mysteries, Classics
General Fiction
Non Fiction and Westerns

Special interest titles available in large print are:
The Little Oxford Dictionary
Music Book, Song Book
Hymn Book, Service Book

Also available from us courtesy of Oxford University Press:
Young Readers' Dictionary
(large print edition)
Young Readers' Thesaurus
(large print edition)

For further information or a free brochure, please contact us at:
Ulverscroft Large Print Books Ltd.,
The Green, Bradgate Road, Anstey,
Leicester, LE7 7FU, England.
Tel: (00 44) **0116 236 4325**
Fax: (00 44) **0116 234 0205**

FIND MADIGAN!

Hank J. Kirby

Bronco Madigan was the top man in the US Marshals' Service — and now he was missing. Working on the most important and most dangerous mission he'd ever been assigned, he'd disappeared into the gunsmoke. Everything pointed to him being one of the many dead bodies left along the bloody trail. Even his sidekick, Kimble, was almost ready to give up the search, but the Chief's orders were very clear: 'Find Madigan . . . at all costs!'

MISFIT LIL GETS EVEN

Chap O'Keefe

While Silver Vein's citizens watch 'Misfit Lil' shine in a gala shooting match, Yuma Nat Hawkins and his gang rob the bank and gun down the depleted opposition in cold blood. Patrick 'Preacher' Kilkieran witnesses the robbery, but keeps his distance — and is soon striking a mysterious deal with a renegade Indian before fleeing town. But it's Kilkieran's brutal assault on Lil's friend Estelle that compels her to vow retribution and track him down . . .

ON THE WAPITI RANGE

Owen G. Irons

When wapiti hunters arrive on Lee Trent's Green River preserve, they bring trouble by carrying too many guns into his peaceful realm. If that weren't enough, they are also holding prisoner a beautiful madwoman in a windowless wagon. The elk hunters' presence threatens to bring Lee into conflict with the Cheyenne Indians, and his neighbours. Then disaster follows when the hunt becomes a slaughter. And Lee must handle the invaders by himself if he is to recover his mountain domain.

ARIZONA SHOWDOWN

Corba Sunman

Travis Jordan was a bounty hunter with his own reasons for turning his back on normal life. Then someone appeared from his past with a plea for help. Family duty reached for him, which he could not ignore, and he returned to his home range. But once he drew his pistol, he would be unable to holster it until the last shot in a bitter clean-up had been fired. It was kill-or-be-killed — and he was resolute that he would win . . .